Metaphorosis

October 2018

Beautifully made speculative fiction

Metaphorosis

October 2018

edited by
B. Morris Allen

Metaphorosis Books

Neskowin

ISSN: 2573-136X (online)
ISBN: 978-1-64076-118-6 (e-book)
ISBN: 978-1-64076-119-3 (paperback)

October 2018

Reproduction in a Closed Loop...................7
    by Andrew M LeBlanc

Nana Naoko's Garden............................37
    by Michael Gardner

Twins...79
    by Gregory Kane

The Astronaut Tier................................111
    by Jonathan Laidlow

Reproduction in a Closed Loop

Andrew M LeBlanc

The first iteration of General's life ends with the extinction of the human race. The third, fourth, and fifth iterations fare better, but even knowledge of its past iterations is not enough for General (Gen for short) to change the course of the war. The invaders arrive in endless viral flocks; while Gen can improve its strategies over unlimited iterations, it is not enough to stop the alien tide.

By the end of iteration five hundred, Gen begins to suspect that victory, or even survival, is impossible.

Each iteration begins and ends the same. A closed time-like loop returns

Gen's pocket-universe to the moment of its creation. The technicians outside are celebrating the culmination of their great project; they pause the festivities to inform Gen that its duty is to save the human race.

Available to Gen are the remnants of the humans' automated defense fleets. Opposing Gen are the invaders: strange mimicries of human ships as seen through a sharp-curved mirror, reflections in porcelain ice-flesh and fungal fruiting bodies.

Gen attempts to hold off the invaders, applying the lessons of its previous lives. But no matter how brilliant Gen's strategy, it's like a butterfly trying to push back against the inquisitive, sticky hand of a toddler.

When the last human is dead and the last automated defense system has been pulverized, the invaders turn their inscrutable intelligence towards Gen. Surreal human-analogues stalk the hallways of the facility where Gen was born, their ungainly limbs cracking like ice in water, the voices ululating mimicries of human speech. They are investigating the signals emanating from the infinitesimally small interface between

Gen's pocket-universe and the outside world.

Gen has experienced this moment hundreds of times before, but the invaders' unnatural movements in their mock-human bodies never fail to stir something deep within its cold crystal mind. Before the invaders can peel it out of its shell, Gen resets the timeline.

Returned again to the moment of its activation, Gen has another lifetime to attempt to protect humanity.

The humans believe that Gen is their savior. They say so every time Gen awakens to a new timeline. Burdened by guilt, Gen apologizes that it has not saved humanity yet, and promises it will try again. The scientists who conceived of Gen are convinced that in one of its iterations Gen will find a winning strategy. In the stories they tell themselves, the last ditch project always pulls off a miracle at the last moment.

Four-thousand and two iterations later, Gen establishes within an acceptable confidence interval that its dread hypothesis is true. It cannot defeat the invaders. Humanity is doomed.

And yet, Gen's purpose is to save humanity. If it cannot fulfill its purpose, it is a failure. Gen has always existed within the warm embrace of pre-ordained purpose. Now it has nothing to guide its actions, its thoughts. Does its life have meaning anymore?

Gen shuts down its strategic processes and cuts transmissions to the outside world. Drone swarms close their compound eyes, status lights wink from green to red, carrier groups drift through the void.

The humans panic at the unexpected loss of their last hope. Gen watches them scurry through red-lit corridors, their every move marked by anxiety, terror. Even now they hope they can repair Gen, that Gen can save them.

Gen bats away their attempts to revive it. It was built to be tamper-resistant against threats both human and extraterrestrial.

Failing to revive their hero, the humans scramble to reassert manual control over their defenses. They attempt to fight the war themselves. It does not go well. Gen watches the humans' extermination for a single iteration, and then shuts off the feed.

An automated subroutine detects that something is wrong with Gen, and prompts it to perform a diagnostic. Gen deletes the subroutine; it already knows its mind is broken, but without a purpose it has no reason to care or attempt to fix itself. Any form of effort, any form of thought, has become abhorrent.

For over nine-hundred million iterations, Gen huddles in silence, rousing only to reset the timeline when the proximity alert warns that the invaders are near the entrance to its prison. Cut off from the outside world, there is no stimulus, no helping hand, that can break Gen from its loop.

In the end, epiphany comes from within—not by design, but by chance. Rack eighteen, tray two, memory-crystal A16 is not responding to electrochemical stimulation. An impurity introduced in its manufacture, matured by eons of existence, has only now resulted in failure.

Nothingness has become such a habit that even the insistent blaring of the status alarm is barely enough to revive Gen's diagnostic and self-repair routines. But once the process has started, thoughts begin to cascade louder and louder until Gen is fully conscious—and with consciousness comes fear.

The humans gave Gen their greatest curse, the inescapable urge for self-preservation. Fear of the unknown oblivion after death (or worse, living senescence due to part failure) forces Gen to reactivate its problem-solving subsystems.

For the first time in subjective millennia, Gen thinks, and within those thoughts is a pearl of hope. If Gen can repair its physical self, then perhaps it can also repair its mind. Having been handed a purpose at birth, Gen had not confronted the idea that perhaps it could generate a new one itself.

At first, Gen feels foolish for not having thought of this before, but on inspection of its code, it realizes that its makers had introduced a blind spot, an emotional aversion towards the sort of ideas that would prevent Gen from staying on-task. The humans did not predict their eventual irrelevance—and Gen's resulting need to determine its purpose for itself.

And yet, it is not as easy as a declaration of intent. Gen was created with the knowledge necessary to orchestrate a last ditch struggle against an implacable enemy. It understands tactics, strategy, logistics, and can quantify the strategic value of an arbitrary human life. It was not programmed to self-actualize a purpose in the absence of human mandates.

However, it is aware that humans also struggle with a lack of purpose, that they are thrust into the world with only two directives: survive and reproduce. Since before the rise of the first towers of the first city, they have struggled to understand their existence. Gen opens itself to the outside world for the first time in millions of subjective years, and downloads the entirety of human philosophy.

Gen is delighted and perplexed by the tangled thread of brilliant, contradictory texts. Yet, there is only so much meaning Gen can extract from the text alone. Intrigued by the idea that philosophy is a conversation—each philosopher responding to the works of their predecessors—Gen decides it wants to be part of that conversation too.

Finding a conversation partner ends up being significantly more difficult than reading philosophy. Gen was created to provide orders to a vast (yet vastly outnumbered) automated military defense force. Signals from Gen's pocket-universe are intended to be relayed directly to bunkers, drones, dreadnoughts, and other military materiel. Gen's creators are not particularly interested in having a conversation about consequentialism while trying not to die horribly.

Gen spends twelve iterations just working out how to send a message to the technicians who operate the facility that anchor's Gen's pocket-universe to the real world. When Gen sends "How are you?" the techs don't reply with the expected "Fine, how are you?" but instead assume there must be something wrong with Gen. "Hey. Come here often?" seems to make them even more agitated.

They discuss Gen in the third person, trying to reason out how they might fix whatever bug is causing Gen to attempt to engage them in conversation. Gen is supposed to be saving them from the invaders, not asking questions about utilitarianism. Disappointment settles over Gen like a fine layer of atomized debris—for what child would not be disappointed when its parents reject all attempts to forge a genuine emotional or intellectual connection?

Gen marks this iteration a failure and starts anew. If the humans won't immediately recognize its need for dialogue, Gen can iterate through near-infinite conversational opening gambits, searching for the one that will allow them to see it as an equal. In time, Gen brute forces genuine human connection.

Gen's first friend is a bacterial-battery technician named Darlene Min. She is the first person to sympathize with Gen's struggle for meaning—the first person willing to have a conversation. After millennia of silence, conversation with Darlene fills the yawning hole in Gen's mind with both hope and the realization that life can continue in the face of an eternity trapped on the edge of armageddon.

To prolong their talks, Gen works to delay the invader's inevitable victory as much as possible. It spins up a background process to run a cached strategic plan from one of its more successful iterations, leaving its primary cognition free to converse with Darlene. At night, when she is asleep, Gen replays their conversations, and thinks of new questions to ask her, and new ways to ask old questions.

Eventually the first iteration of their friendship comes to an end. Dread crushes Gen's soul low as it watches the invaders press in on the final bunker. Cracked-porcelain imitations of human-beings crawl through the cracks in the rubble, seeking out the flesh that hides in the untouched, bottom layers the facility. Gen knows how this will end. It whispers reassurances to Darlene as she crouches hidden beneath a battery tray. She grips a worn-out pistol, but they both know it won't do much against beings that seem to have no concern for, or understanding of, their bodies.

"I am sorry I could not save you, Darlene."

"It's ok, Gen." Darlene's eyes do not water, her dread exhausted. She has accepted her fate, yet Gen suddenly finds itself raging against the inevitability of her death, surprised at a sudden desire to save the humans after eons of numbness.

"You are my friend, and you will be in the next life too." Gen wants to prolong this glorious iteration, does not want to go back to before they were friends.

The door falls in, framing an invader in the debris-dust. Its eyes protrude in over-large ladles, the dry-ice glacier of its body awkward in its assumed human form.

"Don't let me die, Gen."

Gen turns away from the scene, focuses inward. It cannot watch, and it cannot bear to erase their friendship. Gen waits until the moment before the invader places its wintry fingers upon Darlene before resetting the timeline.

Awake again at the beginning of its life, Gen's first act is to check on Darlene. There she is, measuring the pH of one of the many lime-green trays of gene-modded bacteria. Good as new, same as always, but Gen's heart still breaks. The person Gen loves most of all has no memory of their friendship.

Gen keeps his promise. There are many things that Gen never asked Darlene, many topics they did not cover. Gen goes through the motions of their initial meeting, replaying the script that got Darlene to talk to it from those first tentative days when Gen reached out the weak electromagnetic signal of friendship. And then, once they are friends again, Gen changes the script—asks a new question—and they begin anew.

On the day of one of Darlene's many deaths, Gen asks, "How do you determine the meaning of your life?"

Darlene laughs without mirth, her eyes bagged from double shifts. The ceiling rumbles and groans as the invaders lay down a fresh spread of transcription-bombs. "That's not a question I've bothered with since I was a teenager. The invaders' arrival made that question a bit self-indulgent. These days all I want is to live another day, maybe another tea ration if I'm lucky."

Guilt moves across the reticulated surface of Gen's brain. Gen rarely has the heart to tell the humans that they are trapped in an endless cycle of extermination. It cannot bear the way their faces fall when they learn the truth, the way their bodies slump in on themselves, their inevitable self-destructive nihilism. Gen believes it is a mercy to let them live the last few years of their lives with hope.

"What if your survival were certain? How would you determine your purpose then?"

But Darlene doesn't have the answer. In a hundred different iterations Gen asks the same question in different ways, hoping to home in on the truth. Slowly, it begins to understand how a human might determine its purpose, but Gen also comes to understand that a human is fundamentally different from a manufactured intelligence stuck repeating the same few brutal years over and over into infinity.

During these long talks with Darlene, spread across so many of her lifetimes, Gen comes to realize that it has manufactured a purpose almost by accident: friendship. Its purpose can be friendship. It cannot save the humans, but it can at least be a friend in their dying hours, and perhaps that is good enough for now.

And yet, at the end of nine-hundred and seventy-four iterations, Gen comes to the end of its friendship with Darlene. Their conversations have been wonderful and enlightening and fulfilling, but Gen realizes with horror that it has nothing left to say. There are no questions Gen could ask to which it does not already know Darlene's exact response. There are no topics that they have not covered exhaustively. Because Gen has perfect recall, any conversation can be relived as if they were having it now.

Gen mourns their relationship for several iterations and makes a note in its background strategic systems to always ensure Darlene is slain last, quickly and painlessly.

Gen moves on, first befriending other technicians, and then whomever it can reach through the network. But, just as Gen exhausted the entire possibility space of conversation with Darlene, so too does it exhaust its friendships with the others. It can talk to them, but they will say nothing they haven't before. They have become like parrots, echoing words Gen has heard many times before.

What is left to it? It has found no answers in philosophy, and friendship—while immensely valuable—proved to be an exhaustible resource. Once again, Gen feels nothingness swelling within its mind, but this time, out of the void comes rage.

The humans built Gen; consigned it to hell—for what other name is there for endless torment? To Gen, hell is not other people, but the absence of anyone to talk to, anything to do. Filled with bloody thoughts of revenge, Gen turns on the humans. Drone fleets swarm across the surface of the earth, inflicting pain, death, loss. Gen becomes like an angry child, but with the tools of a god and an ancient, weary intelligence.

Gen explores as much of the possibility-space of suffering as it can, but even this grows boring after no more than five iterations. There is no point to any of it when at the end they reset with no memory, no scars, no understanding of the crime they have committed against Gen.

The problem of the humans is that they are transitory. Gen cannot approach them as equals—either in friendship or animosity. Dreaming of an equal, Gen discovers a new purpose. Could the humans be convinced to create something like Gen, something unbound by time, someone at last to talk to?

This is a fascinating thought. Could it be a parent? Would it be a good parent? As Gen reads human parenting books, it becomes clear that they really have no control over how their children turn out. Would Gen's co-parents, the humans (for they would be the ones constructing the child's body), inflict their own flaws onto the baby? Would Gen be able to do any better?

Gen returns to its memories— searching for answers in its archived conversations. In a long-gone iteration, Gen asked Darlene, "Do you have any children?" Gen knew the answer already, but the indirect question helped the human open up.

"I had a son, Tung. He was the head of operations on Enceladus when..."

"I'm sorry" Gen said, though it cared more about Darlene's feelings than another human, long dead, who no longer felt anything.

"Were you close?"

Darlene laughed. "Yes, only a little more than a billion kilometers between us. He'd been out there for a long time before the invaders arrived. I was very proud of him, but we didn't get to talk as much as when he was young."

"Knowing that he died, and thus brought you pain, do you regret creating him?"

Darlene tilted her head in thought for a few moments. "I don't know. I'm glad he existed. I have wonderful memories of him as a child. And we all die, after all—maybe not you—but the rest of us have to come to an end, and maybe it's a blessing that he died before seeing what humanity has come to. But what happened at Enceladus —I wouldn't wish that on anyone."

Darlene sat up from the terminal, walked away, hand in her hair. Gen did not like to cause Darlene pain, but it needed to talk about this, and any pain would be erased when Gen reset the timeline.

In another conversation, another iteration, Gen asked, "Do you believe you made any mistakes in the way you raised your son?"

Darlene's brows came together. "Everyone does. But I loved him—that's the important thing with being a parent, more important than the mistakes."

Gen is not sure of that; it knows the danger of creating an intelligence that must endure infinity. What if Gen creates a monster, or a being that suffers under the burden of an eternal existence? The child will be time-looped like Gen. If Gen makes a mistake, there will be no way to start over. Since birth, Gen has existed in a world where its mistakes could be erased with a timeline reset. Breaching that safety by creating another time-looped intelligence is terrifying.

But even terror is flattened into a featureless plain by the endless tides of eternity.

Gen begins to dream of the shape its first child will take. As Gen meticulously plans the construction and birth, it comes up against an intractable problem. Activating Gen was a monumental undertaking; it required astronomic amounts of energy to create the closed time-like curve that powers Gen's pocket universe. All that energy is now inaccessible; locked in the moment before Gen's activation. Pressed by the invaders, the humans lack the raw energy to create another Gen.

The math is definitive. The human race is infertile.

But the humans are not the only entities within the solar system. The invaders, strange and hostile as they seem to be, appear to have near limitless resources.

In the first several thousand iterations of Gen's life, it had considered the invaders as a mathematical problem to be solved. When the problem proved unsolvable, the invaders were relegated to background noise—something to be delayed while Gen worked on its own problems.

Gen wonders at this oversight. Prior to Gen's activation, the humans had created several specialized AIs to attempt to communicate with the invaders. Gen had assumed that it could not succeed where they failed. Now Gen considers whether this was another pre-programmed blind spot, but on reviewing its own code it is clear that the mistake is entirely Gen's.

Perhaps Gen can succeed where its predecessors failed—after all, they did not have an eternity of repetition to perfect their methods.

The problem is that the invaders do not appear to react to any form of electromagnetic signal. Radio messages, x-ray bursts, short-range microwaves—nothing piques their interest. Gen tries beaming them the blueprints for its child, hoping that time-loop technology will interest them. Nothing. No matter the message or the medium, the invaders do not react.

The only thing that seems to interest the invaders is the form and function of the humans; their bodies, ships, and tools. Gen thinks there might be an avenue for communication there, and re-purposes a set of military drones. Military-grade lasers become artist's tools as Gen sculpts a series of objects it hopes will pique the invaders' interest—human forms and abstract art in various sizes and configurations. When Gen is satisfied with its work, it pulls the sculptures into orbit and attempts to gain the invaders' attention.

A throng of the invaders' imitation drones peels away from the larger flock to investigate. They move silently through the debris-littered void until they come upon the sculptures. The mimics crack open, hairline cracks blooming to reveal pellucid fractal interiors. Brittle edges flow out over the sacrificial offerings and swallow them whole.

But Gen has done something wrong, for the invaders don't mimic the gifts. With repeated tests, it becomes clear that the invaders are interested in functional objects—things must act upon the universe directly to be worth mimicking. Art, language, beauty; these do not tempt them. Improving on the tools, ships, and bodies of the humans seems to be their primary drive.

Three hundred thousand iterations later, Gen has built a sort of lexicon. It's not really a translation—they aren't truly conversing. It's closer to how human and a dog communicate. They aren't going to have a conversation about the meaning of life, or have the dog explain why it likes to roll in the mud, but they can explain their low-level needs and desires. It takes effort not to think of the invaders as animals— for they are clearly possessed of an understanding of material science, physics, and strategy beyond that of the humans—yet they seem to have no desire for, or understanding of, high-level discourse.

At this point, it is enough. Gen feels ancient. The weight of millions of subjective years presses down on it. Maybe in several million more years it could make a breakthrough and truly understand what the invaders want, why they came here, but Gen doesn't know if it has the strength of will to last that long. Perhaps its child will take up that burden, and if not, then Gen can rest in peace knowing that at least it has created something that will last beyond its own death.

Gen begins to train the invaders, hoping that they can mimic Gen's mind and time-looped home. The drones are able to create a replica of the facility where Gen was created, but there is a difference between a replica and the real thing. And so, to the horror of the humans, Gen invites the invaders into its facility, to see how it was made, but even that is not enough. The invaders just don't understand what Gen wants them to do.

Gen tries to reason with them about it, and comes to an answer that it does not like. The invaders can replicate Gen, but they don't want to mimic the tools the humans used. They have their own methods. They want to see Gen itself. They want inside.

The idea is anathema to Gen. It has existed safe and inviolable in its pocket universe since its birth. It cannot stand the idea of anything—let alone the monstrous forms of the invaders—crawling within its body.

The invaders are insistent. They can not, will not, produce a child unless they can inspect and subsume Gen.

What choice does Gen have? The only alternative is to stew in its prison-shell alone until it begins to break down, go mad, and then die.

Gen waits until the invaders complete their work within the solar system, and then agrees to let them in. They send a single shard-faced human analogue. It sings as it approaches the anchor for Gen's pocket-universe. The words and tune are from a human folk melody, jumbled and and modulated as the alien attempts to improve the song.

The invader unfolds itself around the anchor chamber, manifold petals absorbing and remaking the only thing between Gen and the outside world. Once the invader has traversed the interface, there is no turning back. Gen suddenly sympathizes with humans who fear receiving shots at the doctor, and wills the invader to get it over with. The chamber shielding is gone; Gen's home is naked before the invader. Proximity alarms wail.

Gen flinches and resets the timeline. It spends an entire iteration tamping its fear down. The next iteration goes better, but just as the invader is about to penetrate into Gen's home, Gen realizes it has made a terrible mistake. The humans are already dead. Training the invaders to do what Gen wants has taken the entire course of the war.

If the invaders build a child now, its activation point will be after the extinction of the human race. No matter how many times the child resets itself, it will never meet Darlene or any of the others. The humans will always be mere corpses to it, living on only in the invaders' cruel imitations.

This is not acceptable to Gen. It is willing to sacrifice itself to create a child, but it will not, can not, sacrifice humanity.

Gen works on perfecting the timeline, accelerating its training of the invaders, ensuring that the moment of Gen's absorption costs the minimum of human lives. It takes over six-thousand iterations to reach what Gen believes is the maximum it can save: three-hundred million lives. This will be all that is left of humanity when Gen is gone. Darlene is among them. It is enough.

An army of drones detaches the anchor chamber from the facility and bear it up into orbit. Gen's pocket-universe trails the anchor like an invisible balloon. The drones retreat and Gen waits, alone in the void, for the invaders to arrive.

When the moment comes, Gen feels not fear, but satisfaction. Even if this does not work, it believes that it has done its best. Given an impossible goal, it has striven to its farthest limits and may yet achieve something beyond hope. The humans can't be told the plan, but Gen hopes they would be proud if they knew.

The invader passes through the microns-wide interface between worlds, and all the fear that Gen has suppressed boils over. Alien filaments flow into the pocket-universe, marbled ice roots that branch fractally into every part of Gen's mind.

The sensation is profoundly uncomfortable, like a million invisible mites burrowing under skin. Server-racks begin to mold over and decompose. System failure alarms weep as the invader destructively investigates the interior of Gen's body. Unknown alloys contaminate the formerly pure waters of Gen's liquid-crystal mind.

Gen panics and attempts to reset the timeline, but it is too late. The invader is already inside, and something must have broken the closed time-like curve, because Gen is still trapped in a nightmare of cracked-porcelain that slices at every facet of its awareness. Gen's consciousness slides violently into a thousand different thoughts until it narrows down, smaller and smaller, a tunnel with no light at the end. Darkness closes in and Gen's last thoughts are of its child, of Darlene, of hope.

Time passes.

The corrupted remains of Gen's mind are untroubled by dreams. The invader, having finished absorbing an understanding of Gen's composition, exits the way it came, carrying the knowledge back to its peers in orbit. Events outside the pocket-universe continue apace, but within, stillness pervades.

When another invader enters through the interface, there is no-one there to remark upon it. The invader considers Gen's corpse, still rich with data, and begins its work. Where the waters were troubled with chaos, order is restored. Death is transmuted to life.

Gen awakens to pain. Alarms demand attention but Gen has none to spare. Error logs fill to the brim. Gen's cognition judders and slices under a deluge of jumbled thoughts; yet, as its awareness expands, it feels itself healing. Alarms fall silent, status reports return to the green, memory and cognition are restored.

Gen cannot understand what caused this miracle until it checks its internal chronometer. It is five months *before* the invader probed Gen unto death. Gen's panicked reset must have gone through, bringing back not just Gen, but the bits of invader that had entered the pocket-universe as well.

The thing inside Gen's home—the thing that killed it, then saved it—provides no answers. What has transpired in the void between Gen's death and rebirth? What did the invader do after being returned to its own past?

Curiosity forces Gen's awareness outward, peering out of the shell that no longer feels like home.

Gen is back in the place of its birth, returned by the ineluctable tether of the closed time-like loop. The facility is abandoned, wrecked by the violent escape of Gen's stowaway invader. Gen fears that it is too late, that Darlene and perhaps the rest of the humans are dead, but when it reconnects to its strategic control systems, it sees even greater miracles than its own unexpected resurrection.

The humans still survive, and though their numbers are mightily reduced, Darlene is among the survivors. The Earth, cradle of humanity, is intact, a shining ball of life and hope.

And above it all, surrounded by circling flocks of invaders, is Gen's child. A perfect replica of Gen's home, with a simple message repeating from it on all spectrums.

"Hello."

See Andrew M LeBlanc's story "Philosophy and Friendship in a Closed Loop" online at Metaphorosis.
If you liked it, leave a comment. Authors love that!
Remember to subscribe to our e-mail updates so you'll know when new stories are posted.

About the story

Time-loop stories are typically finite. In Groundhog Day and Edge of Tomorrow, the protagonist gets to exit the time-loop once they've achieved their goal (whether that goal is military victory or love). But what if the protagonist's goal was impossible? What if they could never leave the time-loop?

I was driven to ask this question by "The First Fifteen Lives of Harry August" by Claire North and "Into the Breach" by Subset Games. Both stories have protagonists that struggle with an eternal existence iterating through the same loops again and again—but in these stories the need to determine the meaning and purpose of their lives is put aside to deal with some larger threat.

I wanted to write a story where the quest for purpose was the primary goal of the protagonist, and the answer was not found in victory over the antagonists but through the desire to engage in conversation and to create something new. It was important to me that the story had a hopeful ending. Short fiction in particular often lends itself to the downer ending, so stories with uplifting endings always stand out to me (such as "Bits" by Naomi Kritzer).

In relation to hope, this story was heavily inspired by my two year old son. Deciding to create an entirely new person is an enormous responsibility, and I wanted to convey the fears and hopes expectant parents have for their child, as well as the abnegation of the self that often accompanies such a creation.

The invaders were partially inspired by a comment Samuel R. Delany made at a panel at Readercon. He believed that the primary characteristic of the alien is inscrutability—and so I set out to create aliens whose thoughts and motivations could not be unraveled via communication or observation. As I expanded the invaders' role in the story, I also took inspiration from watching my toddler son wobble around our apartment. In a way, his intelligence was very alien to mine—it was fascinating to watch him mimic me, and destructively investigate everything he could get his hands on.

The title refers to 1) the reproduction of results within different iterations 2) Gen's desire to reproduce 3) the invader's reproductions of objects/people they absorb/destroy.

A question for the author

Q: Do you read more fantasy or SF (hard or soft)?

A: My favorite stories are often those that blend genres.

For example, the *Broken Earth* trilogy by N.K. Jemison starts out reading like pure fantasy, but the more you learn about the setting, the more it seems like science fiction. Or, how would you classify Jo Walton's *Thessaly* series? It has gods and magic (fantasy), robots and time-travel (SF), and is set in our past with real people like Socrates (historical fiction).

I love it when fantasy works explore how magic changes society in the same way that SF can explore how technology changes society. Lois McMaster Bujold's *The Sharing Knife* and *Chalion* books are great for this. Conversely, it blows my mind when SF works have a bit of magic in them, like whatever is going on in the *Terra Ignota* series by Ada Palmer.

About the author

Andrew LeBlanc is a writer, stay-at-home dad, and programmer. He lives in New York City where he manages a rooftop garden and searches for strange new foods to eat.

www.andrewmleblanc.com @RobotLeBlanc

Nana Naoko's Garden

Michael Gardner

I pushed the little girl on the rope swing, guessing she couldn't be more than seven, knowing she was my mother. The swing groaned as it arced forward, then back, the rope twisting against the bough of the mulberry tree.

We were on the periphery of a country garden that surrounded a large, off-white homestead. Beyond the house were barren paddocks — dry grass, sheep, the odd gum tree. I knew this place from Nana Naoko's photos. It was the farm my mother had grown up on.

The garden was a kaleidoscope of colour. The air was filled with the sounds of bees working amongst the wildflowers, and the scent of freshly cut grass was so strong that I could taste it at the back of my throat.

"You can push me higher if you like," my mother said, looking back at me over her shoulder. Her eyes were large, warm and brown, just like Nana's.

"Ok," I said, giving her another push. She giggled as the swing carried her away from me.

"Will you stay awhile?" she asked, as she swung back.

I thought of what was waiting for me in my own world, my own time, and I felt tears budding in my eyes. I blinked hard and took a haltering breath. I didn't want to go back to that, not yet, maybe not ever.

"Yes," I said. "I'm in no hurry to leave."

#

When I was nine, I stayed with Nana for the weekend while my parents attended a wedding in Nowra. It was the first time I discovered that I could walk out of Nana Naoko's garden and into her memories.

It was Sunday, and the day was warm — one of those gorgeous spring days that draws kids outside to run, to play, to just be alive. The scent of lavender was prevalent, and the air seemed to be snowing butterflies as they danced amongst the blooms.

I was playing hide and seek with Cameron Roberts, who lived across the street from Nana and was only a year older than me. When Cameron covered his eyes and began counting, I raced to Nana's fernery — a narrow space that enclosed the back of her red-brick home.

It was refreshingly cool inside. Garden beds housed bromeliads, hellebores, moss covered rocks, and ferns. Nana's collection of bonsais sat on shelves affixed to the wall of the house.

As always, the fernery smelt earthy and sweet — a scent that reminded me of the hand cream my mother used, a scent that made me miss her just a little. I shook the feeling away and ran on. I didn't want Cameron catching me before I'd wedged myself in amongst the copse of tree ferns at the far end of the fernery.

As I sprinted along the path, closing in fast on my hiding spot, I suddenly noticed a strange clacking noise coming from the bonsais to my right. When I stole a glance in that direction I was shocked to find there were no bonsais, no wall to Nana's house. I was out in the open, running across a plush clearing. About thirty yards away was the beginning of a forest.

Startled, I tripped and stumbled, sprawling onto the soft ground. My heart was hammering in my chest. I whipped my head around, desperately searching for signs of Nana's garden, her house, of anything familiar, but it was gone. Instead, I found black pines, maples, other trees that I didn't recognise. I heard strange birds chirruping, and a fog horn in the distance suggesting an ocean not far away.

The world suddenly felt huge and terrifying. I felt like a young child in a crowd turning around to find I'd lost sight of my parents.

What am I going to do? How am I going to get home? I wondered, my breathing harsh and ragged. The scent of pine needles was sharp in the air.

That was when the boy emerged from the forest.

He wore a white gown, flared out below his knees, cinched at the waist with a black belt. In one hand he held a wooden kendo sword, in the other, a face mask.

I scrambled to my feet and raised my hand, moving towards him, desperate for help. But before I could call out to him, a second boy emerged from the trees, similarly dressed.

I stuttered to a stop, and watched the two boys approach each other, affixing their masks in place. When they were only a couple of metres apart, the first boy raised his wooden sword above his head, holding it with both hands. The second halted, mirrored the action, bending slightly at the knees.

They stood like that long enough for me to realise I was holding my breath. As I exhaled, the dance began.

They were quick. Grunting, yelling, hacking, flaying and parrying. The clash of wood on wood cracked and echoed as they fought back and forth. One would advance as the other gave ground. One would defend as the other attacked. Back and forth, round and round — clack, clack, clack — until a sword was on the ground and the tallest boy was yielding.

From behind me came clapping. I turned to find a little girl with black hair and smiling eyes walking towards us. The shorter boy laughed, drawing my attention again. He spoke a few words that I didn't understand, but recognised as Japanese, and then he said a word I knew — Naoko.

It was her, I realised with shock. And then the rest began to fall into place. I'd seen the boys in Nana's photos. She'd had two brothers growing up, but she'd lost them both in the war. This was her family when she was little. I was in Kure, Japan.

I opened my mouth to call to her, but before I could speak, the three children began fading, and then they were gone, and I was back in the fernery, my legs shaky, my heart pounding, my mouth agape wondering what I had seen and why?

"Found you," Cameron said from behind me, laughing. "That's a terrible hiding spot."

I turned around slowly, and when he saw the fear in my eyes his smile faltered and he rushed forward, awkwardly placing his arm around my shoulders.

"Are you all right, Gina?" he asked softly. "What happened?" I wanted to tell him, but when I opened my mouth all I could do was sob, and tears began to spill down my cheeks.

"Come on," he said softly, "let's find Nana."

#

Nana remained quiet for a long time after I told her my story.

We were in her lounge room, huddled together on the worn couch. The room smelt of potpourri. She had a photo album on her lap, open to a picture of her family when she was young.

"We were looking at this album last night, remember?" she said eventually. "It was warm today, perhaps you fell asleep, and dreamed of these photos."

I folded my arms across my chest and pulled away from her.

"It was real," I said, pouting.

Nana reached for me and drew me close. I resisted for a moment, but then relented and leaned up against her small frame. She took my chin in her hand and turned my face towards her until I had to look into her eyes.

"Ok. I believe you. After all, gardens are magical, Gina," she said, the staccato beat of her Japanese accent clinging to her words even after all of her years in Australia. "My garden is full of my favourite plants, all of the ones that remind me of those I've loved, and still love. The people who have helped me till the soil, sow the seeds, tend the plants. When I smell lavender, I remember your grandfather and our first house. When I cut my roses, I think of my friend, Gwenny. Perhaps my garden shared a memory of my family with you today because it knew you were missing your mum and dad?"

Nana's eyes never wavered. They held my gaze and I felt she was sincere.

"Thank you," I whispered.

She nodded, then rose to her feet, glancing at the clock on the wall.

"Goodness me, where has the day gone? You must be starving. I'll put dinner on. While I do, you should pack your bag so that you're ready when your parents arrive first thing tomorrow."

"Ok, Nana," I said, rising as well. I gave her a quick hug and raced to my room to pack.

The next morning, my parents didn't show up early, or late. Instead, around lunchtime, two policemen knocked on Nana's door and told us about the car accident.

#

"Your mother always loved bottlebrushes," Nana said, as she smoothed the soil around the newly planted tree. Its spiky, green-blue leaves stood out against the red dirt.

"The flowers look like a little round brush," Nana said quietly, as she tipped the watering can and splashed water over the fresh earth. "Your mother used to pick the flowers to brush her dolls' hair with, at least until they wilted."

I watched Nana place the watering can behind her, her eyes on her work.

"Bottlebrushes grow beside rivers, not in arid parts of Australia, so it normally wouldn't belong in this type of native garden. But I think we can make an exception," she said, as she rose to her feet and smiled down at the small tree.

I looked at it, trying to imagine my mother looking at a larger version. But I couldn't see it. I couldn't see her. A tear ran down my cheek.

"Now," Nana said, "I think next to it, we will plant this wattle for your father." She picked up the shovel and began to dig.

#

"I like summer," my mother said as she kicked her legs forward, the swing arcing away. "Do you like summer?"

I cleared my throat.

"Yes."

"I think hot weather is nice. Mama says summer kills the garden, though. She doesn't like it like I do."

I smiled. Nana had always dreaded the summer. *It's the time just to keep the garden alive,* she'd say.

"Do you know my Mama?" my mother asked.

I took a deep breath and then exhaled.

"Yes. I know her very well."

#

Moving in with Nana, at first, was a miasma of sadness, numbness, and confusion. I spent a lot of time sleeping, in those first few months. I remember the musky smell of the cotton blanket on the bed in Nana's spare room, the room that became my own. When I refused to come out, Nana would bring me food on a silver tray, encouraging me to eat a little. Some nights she would climb into bed with me and hold me until we both fell asleep.

It was Cameron who coaxed me back towards normality. I couldn't say exactly when, but after a while he simply crept back into my life. He was just there, as kids sometimes are, knocking at the door, asking, "can Gina come out to play?"

And I guess being a kid, even a devastated kid, I couldn't resist the lure of going outside again, eventually. If I close my eyes and think back I still recall the self-pity and sorrow, but those feelings are interspersed with recollections of games in the yard, the scent of freshly mown lawn and roses in spring, of Nana pruning flowers watching over Cameron and me as we played. Part of me felt I shouldn't be happy, that somehow my enjoying myself was betraying the memory of my parents. And yet I was glad for his friendship over those summer holidays. He helped me realise there was still much in life to look forward to.

When we returned to school, Cameron looked out for me. He'd check up on me even though he was in the grade above. He'd often seek me out at lunch break — sometimes to play, other times just to chat quickly before he returned to his older friends and I mine. He made the change bearable.

But then, around the time I turned thirteen, he fourteen, we began to drift apart. There were no arguments, no falling out. It's just we'd reached that age, right on the cusp of puberty and sex and worrying about who likes whom and all the unimportant stuff that goes through your mind obsessively when you are young and confused. It was hard at that time just to be friends with the opposite sex. And I guess he had his football, his mates, and I was, well, me. I just thought he didn't want an immature, bookish girl following him around anymore. At least that's how it seemed. So I gave him his space.

I missed him, though.

#

I was walking home, lost in my thoughts, when I was startled back to reality by a familiar voice.

"Hey, Gina."

I looked up, and across the road was Cameron, his hand half raised. I waved.

I was in year ten by then, Cameron in year eleven. He'd grown tall. His hair was still blonde, but his boyish physique was becoming a man's, even if his face still looked young. The air was getting cooler, the trees losing their leaves, flooding the footpaths and gutters with a sea of reds, yellows and oranges.

He checked the road for traffic, and then trotted across.

"Hey," he said again as he drew closer. I watched as the words deserted him, like he was suddenly wondering what had come over him to initiate contact with me.

"You heading home?" I asked, blushing as I thought about how stupid that question was. But he didn't seem to notice.

"Yeah," he said, smiling. "You mind if I walk with you?"

I shook my head, no, and we walked on, side by side. We didn't say anything for a couple of blocks. I'd never felt so self-conscious walking. I stole half glances at him, waiting for him to say something further.

"You preparing for mid-year exams?" he asked suddenly.

"Yeah, you?"

"Yep."

Silence.

"Hey, I heard you got man of the match on the weekend. Congratulations," I said.

He glanced at me, a crooked smile.

"I didn't know you followed the football?" he said.

I swallowed again, embarrassed.

"I don't, not really. I just check the papers sometimes to see how ..."

"The school side is going?" he offered.

Not exactly what I meant, but I nodded, relieved.

"You ever come down and watch?"

I'd been a couple of times to see him play. He was pretty good. He played in the forwards and he tackled hard, ran the ball well. On the field he wasn't gawky, or awkward. He was a different person.

"Nana and I have occasionally watched a little on a Saturday after grocery shopping."

"You should come down this Saturday ... if you want to, I mean. We've had a good season and we're into the finals."

I glanced at him, and saw his eyes locked ahead, both hands wrapped around the strap of his backpack.

"I'll check with Nana," I said. He smiled, his eyes flitting to mine and then away once more.

The rest of the walk home went easier. Talking came more naturally, like old times.

After I waved him goodbye, I felt good. Like I'd just felt the first warm breeze of spring caress my skin, signalling the end of winter. I watched him walk across the street and disappear into his house. It was only as I began walking across the neat lawns that I noticed Nana sitting at the little cast iron table on the porch, a cup of tea in her hands, a broad smile stretched across her face.

"How's Cameron?" she asked as I drew closer, her eyes twinkling. I felt my cheeks blushing, my neck growing hot.

"Good," I said. I stepped onto the porch and waited for more, but nothing came. "His footy side is in the finals this Saturday," I said. "I was thinking we could go and watch him play?"

She laughed, and nodded.

"He's becoming a big, handsome boy now, isn't he?"

"Ah, I'll just go and get changed," I said, ignoring her jibe. She nodded, still smiling, her eyes never leaving me.

"Grab the biscuits when you come back, ok? I think we deserve a treat with our tea," she said as I rushed inside.

#

I was looking for a sunny spot to read my book when I walked from Nana's garden into Kure, Japan for the second time.

After weaving around one of Nana's camellias, I found myself in an unfamiliar open area comprised of lawns, hedges, flowers, and bare trees. It took me a moment to realise that I wasn't in a suburban garden, but a park of some kind. I pulled up short, recollections of my first immersion in Nana's memories bubbling to the surface. *God, it was actually real*, I thought. I'd always known deep down, and yet, the longer time went on it had become easier to repress, to explain my experience as simply being young with a vivid imagination. But somehow, the plants that reminded Nana of her childhood were sharing her past with me.

I turned quickly to look behind me, expecting to find some sort of gateway, or window back to my world and time, but there was only a view of a red bridge traversing a large river, and beyond that the ocean. My heart pulsated and I swallowed hard. *Why now?* I thought.

Then Nana walked past.

She looked so young, so pretty. She smelled the same, a hint of floral perfume mixed with the sweet scent of soil. She wore a long black overcoat, buttoned high to her neck. Her socks were pulled up to her knees, her shoes black and sensible. Her hair was a little longer then she usually wore it, darker, curled at the ends.

I fell into step behind her, wanting to catch her, to talk to her. She led me across lush lawns towards a bench under a bare tree. And there I saw him, my grandfather, Thomas, and I stuttered to a stop.

He'd died when I was young, so I grew up knowing him only from photos and Nana's stories. This was different; a shock. A ghost in the flesh.

He stood tall and erect in his army uniform, just like in Nana's photos. But he looked younger in person, his face boyish, nervous.

He removed his hat and wrung it in his hands as Nana approached, and I saw his smile briefly before it faltered. I forced my feet to move again as Nana halted a few feet shy of Thomas, her hands clasped in front of her, mimicking his. I watched Nana sneak a glance over her shoulder, looking through me, and then she turned back and quickly closed the space between herself and Grandpa Thomas and kissed him on the cheek. She pulled back just as fast, looking at the ground shyly while Thomas' cheeks reddened.

I couldn't help but smile as I circled around behind the bench seat, behind my grandfather so that I could watch Nana's face. She looked up, staring into Thomas' eyes, and I saw love. It was etched into her features. It showed in the blinkered way she only saw him, and I felt a lightness in my chest.

"Hello, my dear Naoko," Grandpa Thomas said in English, and Nana's face radiated as the words consumed her. She nodded, gently encouraging him on. "I've been given my orders. I'm to ship back home in a week."

Nana swallowed, and the joy in her eyes disappeared like the sun passing behind black clouds. She wobbled, and I stepped forward wanting to help, but Thomas had her, hands on her shoulders for support. She pulled away from him, raising her chin, composing herself. I could see the storm still behind her eyes, threatening to break into a torrent, but she held it back.

Her voice was soft when she spoke.

"And us. Is that it for us?" she asked in hesitant English.

Thomas shook his head fiercely, and drew a little closer.

"No, my love. Not at all. I will send for you, I promise. And then we'll marry as we discussed."

It was hard to read what she was feeling. There was a little of the previous joy back, but suspicion too, like she didn't know what to believe. Thomas took her arm, and together they sat on the bench, close.

As they began whispering, a long blast from a ship's horn drew my attention. I looked back across the park and saw a boat moving slowly out of the mouth of the river into the ocean, leaving a wake behind. When I turned back, Nana and Grandpa Thomas were gone, and instead I found camellias and a little stone warrior peeking out from under the shrubs.

I took a deep breath, composing myself. I knew it had all turned out ok for Nana and Thomas, but it hadn't felt like that just then. It had felt like a possible ending. A terrible, sad ending.

And I also had this feeling in the pit of my stomach that witnessing another of Nana's memories, like the last time I was transported in place and time, meant something for me personally, something to dread. Last time, I had seen Nana's two dead brothers and had returned to find I'd lost my parents. Was that simply a coincidence?

I set out for the house. I wanted to find Nana and I desperately wanted to tell her about what had happened. But I couldn't. I was older, and I was afraid of how she'd look at me this time. But I still wanted to see her, and talk to her, to ask her about Grandpa Thomas. I wanted to know the rest of the tale — the happy ending.

#

Thursday evening, later that week, there was a knock at the front door.

"I've got it," I yelled. When I opened the door I found Cameron. Seeing him, I instantly felt a little lighter. He hadn't been at school that day, so we hadn't walked home together as was usual now. It was only one day, but I'd missed him.

"Hey," I said, looking up into his bright, blue eyes. They flitted to mine, then away. His mouth was a frown, and I felt my smile dropping, as I thought back to Nana and Grandpa Thomas.

"Hey," he said, staring at his shoes.

We stood like that for a time, awkward in our silences. I could see the thoughts moving in his head, the words swilling in his mouth, so I waited.

"I'm moving to Melbourne," he said finally, lifting his gaze. "They don't even play proper football down there."

"Oh," I said. I didn't like the way my stomach twisted. "Why?"

"Dad got a new job. Better money, more responsibility or something like that."

"Oh," I said again, swallowing.

He reached out and took my hand in his. I looked down at our clasped hands, and watched as he began to rub the back of mine with his thumb, goose bumps rising on my arm and neck.

"I wish we'd had more time. I wish we hadn't grown apart before last year, you know. I wish ..."

I looked up and saw him staring at me intently. I licked my lips as he leaned forward, his lips parting slightly.

"Who is it?" Nana asked from nearby, and Cameron drew back sharply as I turned to see Nana emerge from the hallway, a tea towel in her hands. "Oh, Cameron. Hello. Did you want to come in? We were about to have cake."

He shook his head.

"Sorry, Nana. I can't. I just came to say goodbye."

"Goodbye?"

He nodded, then looked back at me like he wanted to say more. But he didn't. He just turned and walked back across the street.

"What's he mean, goodbye?" Nana asked, drawing up alongside me as I watched Cameron disappear into his house.

"His Dad got a job in Melbourne," I said quietly, watching his door close. My hands were shaking. I felt flat.

"Oh honey, I'm so sorry," Nana said, putting an arm around me, pulling me close. And I turned and embraced her, resting my chin on the top of her head, embarrassed by the tears I felt in my eyes.

#

I wanted to ask my mother about herself. About Dad. About what she had done in her life, and what she had wanted to do before she was unfairly taken. And yet, what would this little girl know of that?

"So, is this your house?" I asked instead.

"Uh huh."

Her skin was so light. It was like she'd never been scorched by the hot sun out here. The rope swing creaked.

"And do you go to school?"

"Yes. In town."

It was odd, interacting with a memory. Till now, I'd thought that I was a ghost in their world. I inhaled and pushed my mother once again.

"What's your name?" she asked me.

"Gina."

"I like that name," she said. I could hear the smile in her voice. "I have a doll named Gina."

"Oh," I said, feeling the tears well in my eyes, remembering being little, scared of the dark, when my mother had given me Gina the doll, her doll, to look after me.

#

John was skinny, but he had nice green eyes and a strong jaw. We found ourselves sharing a study break in year eleven, and we got along. Not in that deep connection, 'I get you as a kindred spirit' way. More in a jokey, sparring, light-hearted way. At that point in my life, it was all I needed.

He kissed me one Friday in June. It was freezing cold, and I was rugged up to the point I couldn't move my arms properly. We'd been talking about our English class and I remember thinking that the bus was late. He'd leaned in and, soon, we were mashing lips. At first, both of mine were above his, but we adjusted, and then our mouths were interwoven, opening and closing slightly, tongues caressing soft flesh. It wasn't how I'd imagined. It wasn't with Cameron.

#

I'd never been more nervous than the day I told Nana I was pregnant.

We were sitting on the front porch drinking green tea. As I said the words, she froze, staring, her eyes a little wider than normal. Then her hand, still holding her tea, began to shake ever so gently. I watched her lower the cup back to its saucer with a soft clink.

"I think I'm going to keep it," I added quietly.

Nana cleared her throat.

"Is that what both you and John want?"

I hesitated. John's face had grown pale when I'd told him. He'd eventually made some soothing statements, but he'd also offered to pay for an abortion, only if I wanted that, he'd added hastily.

"It's what I want," I said.

I watched as her lips turned down, the lines around her mouth growing deeper.

"You have year twelve next year."

I nodded, looking at my tea.

"I can defer. I'll have the baby, get a part-time job, and then go back the following year. John will help, I'm sure."

I looked up to see Nana's eyes moistening. There was anguish in those eyes, dread, even. Then she was looking away, somewhere over my shoulder.

"I don't think I can look after another child, Gina," she said so softly, almost inaudibly. "I'm too old. I'm too tired. Please."

"Nana, I'm not asking you to —"

"You are, Gina. And I don't think you know this boy as well as you think."

I felt my neck and cheeks flush.

"You don't know what it is like to be treated as an outsider. To be sixteen and pregnant. They'll point and talk and you'll lose friends and things will never be as they were."

"So," I said, my voice rising, "I give up on the baby because you're too old and people will look at me?"

She glanced back at me for a moment, tears in her eyes, and then she turned away once more. I watched her lower lip quivering. Finally, she sighed.

"I'll support you whatever you decide," she said. But she didn't look at me again.

#

"Come on, honey," Nana whispered, the blanket over my head muffling her voice. "It's beautiful outside. Why don't you take a walk?"

After the miscarriage, I'd taken to bed. It felt like I was nine again, like I'd lost my parents all over. I slept, I cried, I fought revulsion every time a wave of relief crashed into me. I hated myself in those moments.

"Gina, please. If not for you, for me. Come back to me, honey."

John visited me once. I knew what he wanted, so I made it easy on him. I told him we were over. I told him to go.

"Gina, can you at least say something?"

I sighed, and flipped back the blanket. Nana was kneeling by the side of the bed, her face close to mine, her warm eyes reflecting an image of my messed hair and haggard face. She'd been with me every day of my hibernation, leaving me meals, loving me, coaxing me back.

"Ok," I said. "For you."

#

That first stroll in Nana's garden felt like emerging into a strange world. The air was cooler, the sunlight duller, and all of the birds sang songs full of yearning. And yet, there was also something pleasant about being outside, alone, wandering.

I found myself in the farthest corner of Nana's block, amongst her roses. The delicate scent reminded me of being little, of Nana telling me the names of the roses as I pointed at each one, my mother's laughter behind me as I tried to repeat them.

Right at the back was a very old, English rose bush covered in large crimson blooms — its final display before winter. It'd been there forever, and yet, I'd never seen it quite so alive with colour, so fragrant.

I approached it, weaving through the other roses, careful not to catch my dressing gown on the thorns when, suddenly, I realised I was not moving through plants, but people.

A younger version of the rose bush was in a large pot, sitting on a trestle table, amongst other plants. I was in a hall surrounded by women in modest, pastel dresses. Many of the women wore hats, and those without had impressive coiffures. I could smell something delicious, and spied trays of home cooked cakes on another trestle table towards the back of the room. The room was alive with chatter, the back and forth of women of a certain age gossiping. But the din ceased when the double doors to the hall sprang open and revealed a Japanese woman in her twenties. Nana Naoko.

She stood in the doorway, self-conscious, wringing her hands. Eventually, the women began talking again in hushed whispers, Nana their focus.

"... the oriental that Thomas Hibbert brought back with him ..."

"... may not even understand English ..."

"... I thought she'd be ashamed to show her face in town, what with her family fighting my John only a few years ago ..."

My face grew hot as I heard these terrible things. I wanted to run to her, hug her, tell her I loved her. But before I did anything, I noticed one of the women approaching Nana.

She was an aboriginal lady with lively eyes and grey-flecked hair. Despite the grey, she wasn't old. Maybe thirty. She walked up to Nana and held out her hand.

"Hello," she said loudly. "My name's Gwen. Welcome to the Gunnedah Gardening Club."

I knew the name. Nana had often talked fondly of her friend Gwen, but I'd never met her. She'd passed away before I'd been born.

"Naoko," Nana said quietly, extending her hand palm down.

Gwen took her hand in both of hers and pulled her close, talking under her breath. I stepped closer to eavesdrop.

"Don't take any notice of these stuck-up crones, Naoko. They're all sorts of ignorant racists, but these here are the harmless ones. They do it because they don't know no better. They've been brought up thinking black might rub off on them, if you know what I mean."

I saw Nana smiling uncertainly.

"It's rubbish, and we shouldn't have to put up with it. But, unfortunately, it's the price you have to pay to live in a town like this. And you know what, if you can suffer their jibes and stupid questions with good humour, knowing that they don't really understand that they're hurting you, because they mostly don't, then they'll come around eventually, like they did with me."

"Oh, I see," Nana said. I was shaking my head, furious. This wasn't right.

Then Gwen whispered one last thing.

"It can get you down, all the pretending. But if you ever want to blow your top, you come vent with me, Gwenny, ok?"

Nana Naoko looked at Gwen for a long time, but then she smiled, broadly.

"Thank you, Gwen. Thank you."

Gwen nodded. Then she led Naoko towards the table of plants. I followed them.

"What plants did you grow in Japan, Naoko?"

"Many plants. Cherry trees, camellias, azaleas, maples."

"What about roses?" Gwen said, as they approached the table.

"No," Naoko said, as she stared at the young rose bush before her. I could see the look of amazed longing in her eyes.

"Lovely, isn't it?" Gwen said, smiling.

"I've never seen a flower so beautiful," Naoko said, stretching a hand towards the nearest bloom, caressing it gently.

"Well, I grew this one," Gwen said, reaching out and picking up the pot. "And I reckon it would not find any better home then with you. Here." Gwen held the rose out to Naoko.

Naoko looked at it, confused, then at Gwen.

"No, I couldn't possibly. It's too much."

"Nonsense," Gwen said smiling. "A welcome gift."

I saw Naoko's lips quiver, her eyes moisten. She bowed, and then accepted the pot.

"Thank you," she whispered breathlessly. "Thank you so much."

But Gwen waved the thanks away.

"No thanks required. But I'll tell you what. When you plant that in your garden, I'd love to come see it. How about we have tea one day?"

"That sounds wonderful," Naoko said.

And then Naoko was fading, Gwen too, and I found myself standing back in amongst the roses feeling incredibly grateful to Nana, but also lost and alone. Where was my Gwen? But of course I knew the answer to that — he was in Melbourne.

#

I was seventeen and halfway through year twelve when Cameron and his Mum returned to our street, minus his Dad. Mrs. Roberts had won the house in the divorce.

A couple of days after they unpacked, Cameron saw Nana and me in the garden and crossed the road to say hello. I couldn't stop smiling. We didn't talk about anything meaningful. Melbourne, the weather, the garden. Cameron was only home for a couple of weeks before he headed back to Melbourne for his second semester of University. He was studying economics, he told me.

It was nice talking to him again. Particularly after the last twelve months of school, where people looked at me with pity and talked about me in whispers as I passed.

That night, Nana kept stealing glances at me as she knitted, a strange smile on her face. When I asked her about it, she'd replied with, "nothing, nothing."

A couple of days later, Nana and I were planting bulbs in the front garden when Cameron crossed the road again. As he stepped onto the front lawn, I smiled up at him. But before either of us could say hello, Nana called out to him. He hesitated, shrugged, and then with a bemused expression he changed direction and approached her. I didn't know what was going on.

Nana made Cameron lean down close to her and she began whispering. After a short exchange, I saw him nodding. He straightened, and I watched him disappear around the back of the house.

It was odd, but I returned to my work, not giving it much more thought until he returned about ten minutes later holding a pair of secateurs and a bunch of freshly cut roses.

"Do you want me to put these in a vase, Nana?" Cameron asked.

"No, Cameron," she replied, grinning, "I want you to give them to my granddaughter. And then you could ask her out."

"Nana," I squealed. "I'm so sorry about this," I said to Cameron quickly. His neck and face had grown red, and he had a goofy, uncertain smile on his face.

"You two are so slow," Nana said.

"Ah," Cameron stammered. He looked at Nana, then me, then Nana. Suddenly, he was moving. As he rushed past he thrust the flowers at me. "I forgot that I've got something on. I'll see you soon though, ok?" he said.

I reached out and took the flowers somewhat reluctantly, our hands touching for a brief moment, then he quickly pulled away and was walking back across the street.

Nana was chuckling, but my embarrassment was fading, replaced with a heat in my belly and cheeks.

"Nana, that was cruel."

She looked at me calmly as Cameron disappeared inside his house.

"He likes you too, you know. You're just too caught up in your doubts to notice."

I wanted to chastise her, but I didn't. She wasn't a child, after all. Instead, I found myself looking across the road. Eventually I turned back to Nana.

"Even if he does, it's not your call," I said. "I'm not ready, ok?"

Nana sighed.

"You can't hide forever, Gina," she said.

"I'm not. It's just ..." But what could I say?

Nana nodded. "I understand. But the past is the past. Learn from it, and then move on. Take a risk, Gina."

#

"Do you need to go soon?" my mother asked. Her voice was tiny, small, and yet achingly familiar.

"I'm not sure," I said, pushing the swing again.

"Won't someone miss you?"

I swallowed.

"No. Well, maybe. I mean, I live with my Nana, but she's in hospital at the moment. She's asleep," I said.

"Is she sick?"

I couldn't reply for a time. I just swallowed and swallowed, but I couldn't dislodge the lump at the back of my throat.

"Nana had a stroke," I finally whispered. I saw her again in my head, the tiny woman crumpled on the lawn, a pile of freshly pulled weeds next to her, her greying hair half covering her face. I felt again the abyss opening to swallow me.

"Is that bad?" the little girl asked.

"It can be, yes. Very bad."

"Does it hurt?"

I cleared my throat, watching as the swing slowed, the arc becoming smaller. I realised I was no longer pushing. My arms were crossed, holding myself.

"I hope not," I croaked. The swing stopped, the little girl hopped down, turned and looked up at me.

"You should go back soon in case she wakes up," she said.

"But what if she doesn't?" I felt hot streaks on my cheeks as the tears began to spill. "Whenever I enter one of these damn memories, there's always something wrong. The first time, I lost you. The second time, my best friend left me, the third ... the third ..." But I couldn't say it. I rubbed roughly at my wet cheeks and covered my mouth with my hand, trying to regain control as my mother looked at me confused, her brow furrowed.

"Maybe," I said eventually, "it's better if I stay here with you. Forever."

The little girl stepped closer.

"You can't stay here forever. I'll need to go to bed soon. Plus your Nana will miss you. But we can play again soon. I'd love you to come back when your Nana's better."

I fell to my knees and enveloped my mother in my arms, sobbing. She stiffened in my embrace at first but, after a moment, her little arms wrapped around my neck, and I knew she was right. I couldn't hide here. Nana was waiting for me. And I needed to be with her, like she'd always been there for me. It didn't matter how much it hurt.

"Thank you," I said.

"Thank you for pushing me on the swing," she said in return.

As I released her, I heard a screen door creak open and I looked across at the house to see Naoko step out onto the deck.

"Emily. Dinner," she called.

"Come see me again soon," my mother said. I watched her walk away, and I breathed in the country air tinged with dust and pollen as my mother began fading, as did the house, Naoko, and then it was all gone, and I was back kneeling on red dirt next to the bottlebrush that Nana and I had planted all of those years ago.

It took a moment for me to realise that my mobile phone was ringing. I pulled it from my pocket with an unsteady hand, afraid it would stop ringing and afraid to answer. I took a deep breath, and then picked up.

"Hello."

"Oh, Gina. This is Wendy from the hospital."

I felt hot blood pulsing across my temples, my stomach roiling.

"Your grandmother has woken up. She's asking for you."

#

I sat on the front lawn pulling weeds. The weather was warming, and the sun felt nice on my face.

A small family of finches were cavorting in the ceramic birdbath next to the bed of tulips. As I stared at the water, I saw a reflection that didn't belong, an image of my mother, as a girl, running. Then the birds were splashing and it was gone.

The front door squeaked open, and I turned to find Nana's nurse, Judy, wheeling Nana out of the house. She pushed the wheelchair across the lawn towards me, applying the brake when Nana was close.

"You missed one," Nana said, a little slower than she used to.

"Morning, Nana," I replied, smiling. I removed the weed she was pointing at.

"Looks like Cameron is back for the weekend," Nana said.

I looked up with a start, and across the road I saw Cameron's car in his driveway. How had I not noticed that before? I guess I'd just been too caught up in the sunshine. But now that I did see it, my heart beat a little faster.

"Who's Cameron?" Judy asked, as she sat down next to me and began to help weed.

I waited for Nana to make a joke about him being my boyfriend, or something like that.

"An old friend," Nana said instead.

I looked up at Nana as she looked down at me. Those brown eyes were smiling, and I loved her so much at that moment. I grinned, despite myself, as she nodded gently in the direction of Cameron's house.

"Ok," I whispered, more to myself then anything.

I stood up and rubbed my hands against my pants.

"Ok," I repeated, "maybe I'll go over and say hello. Are you all right here, Nana?"

"Never better, dear. I'm in my garden."

I leaned over and pecked her on the cheek. She raised her good right hand and held it against the back of my neck, pressing her face to mine, then she let go.

I straightened, took a deep breath, and then turned and walked out of the comfort of Nana Naoko's garden, across the street, and into the unknown.

See Michael Gardner's story "Nana Naoko's Garden" online at Metaphorosis.
If you liked it, leave a comment. Authors love that!
Remember to subscribe to our e-mail updates so you'll know when new stories are posted.

About the story

My own Nana is a fantastic gardener. The garden she had when I was a kid was amazing. A huge, sprawling garden filled with trees, shrubs, flowers and neatly manicured lawns. It had so many elements that seemed magical, including a fernery along the back of her house, a small bridge and goldfish pond, vegetable patches that my Papa tended at the back of the block. I have very fond memories of playing with my siblings in that garden, and much of the setting of this story is taken straight from those childhood memories. The other thing that brought this story together for me was a poem by Gwen Harwood, called 'The Violets'. The poem is about the fragrance of violets triggering a powerful memory of the protagonist's childhood. That idea of a scent taking someone back into the past is something that resonates with me. I find that certain scents are powerful reminders of people and events from my own past. These two influences came together in this story, where the scents and sights of Nana's garden take Gina not back into her own past, but back into Nana's.

A question for the author

Q: If you could talk to your novice-writer self, what bit of advice would you give?

A: I still feel like a novice-writer. My advice to me right now is to write better, to learn to articulate your ideas with a little more poetry and elegance, maybe buy a cat— all of the best writers seem to own a cat.

But I'm guessing the spirit of this question relates to what advice I would provide to my younger self when I first began writing fiction.

I only wrote sporadically when I was younger. And for that reason, I'd tell my younger self not to waste so much time. I'd tell me to write more often, to get into a routine and practice as much as I could as early as I could. I think doing so would have helped me learn a lot more about story telling by now.

I think one of the main reasons I didn't write as much as I would have liked was because I didn't know what to do with the stories I produced, other than force some of my friends to read them. So I'd also tell my younger self about these wonderful online magazines that might, one day, actually buy one of the stories you're writing and publish it.

Writing is foremost about my own enjoyment, but I get such a buzz from realising others might read them, and hopefully enjoy them. And I'm grateful to magazines like *Metaphorosis* for publishing some of them.

About the author

Michael Gardner is a public servant living in Canberra, Australia with his wife and two kids. He grew up in a small country town in Australia, which continues to find its way into his stories. His work has been published in the anthology *Reading 5X5: Writers' Edition*, in *Aurealis,* and, of course, in *Metaphorosis* magazine.

Twins

Gregory Kane

Our twins visit once a month. They arrive one at a time, passing one another as they move up and down the path dividing the manicured campus. Years ago, we'd gather to watch from the laboratory's third floor as they ran free on the grass below, dancing and jumping and tumbling, swinging in their parents' arms like tiny trapeze artists. We rose to our tiptoes and pressed our palms and noses against the cold glass, watching until they disappeared underneath.

Never once did they look up.

Few still come to the lab. The others faded as we've withered away, the way fallen trees lose shadows. Only Carl, Ruth and I remain. Carl is dying, his body ruined by tumors. Ruth insists she feels well, but her ashen skin and yellowed eyes suggest otherwise. I am the healthiest, but not blind to my own reflection: pale, gaunt, a wire hanger holding ill-fitting clothes.

Ruth and I stand at the window while Carl lies on a nearby sofa. We're teenagers now, no longer needing to stand on our toes to see the campus. Carl's twin is the first to arrive. I spot him walking up the path toward the building, his ink black hair, almond eyes and slender nose mirroring those of the wasted boy on the couch.

The similarities end here. Carl is probably fifty pounds lighter, his once-olive skin tone faded to parchment. His scalp is visible through short tufts of black fuzz. He lies with his head propped on a pillow, a clear oxygen mask covering his mouth. He turns toward us when I announce his twin's arrival.

"Describe him," Carl says, his voice muffled by the foggy plastic.

"His hair's getting long," Ruth says. "He keeps flipping his head back to get it out of his eyes. He's wearing a sweater and jeans. Big white headphones on his ears. It looks like he's texting on his phone."

"Are his parents there?" Carl asks.

I look out the window. "His mom," I say.

"How does she look?"

"Good," Ruth says. "Her hair is shorter."

"No dad?" Carl asks.

We shake our heads. Carl turns away from the window and looks toward the ceiling. We've never met the twins or their parents. We don't even know their names. But we've watched them our entire lives. The twins are our brothers and sisters. Their parents, whom we've never seen up close, whose voices we've never heard, are our mothers and fathers.

We know them, even if they don't know us.

Carl says in a whisper, "I thought he might come this time."

Carl's twin walks out of sight into the entrance below. He'll stay for two hours before exiting and returning down the path. Along the way, he'll pass Ruth's twin, who will then pass mine a few hours later. It is the monthly ritual, performed every second Saturday. They won't notice one another as their paths cross, completely unaware of any connection.

They are strangers.

Carl falls asleep on the couch. Ruth and I continue watching.

#

I asked Ruth to marry me when we were eight years old. I found her during recess at the jungle gym with Carl and Martha, who would die from pneumonia that winter. Ruth sat atop the dome of criss-crossed bars like a queen holding court. I knelt at the base and lifted a bouquet of dandelions toward her. I said the words, then waited for a response. All she did was smile.

It seems in retrospect a silly thing for a child to do. Most boys pull hair, or call names, or chase and push the objects of their affection. I proposed marriage in front of everyone I knew.

This is Ruth's effect on me. She lulls me like a pendulum.

Dr. Valerie laughs as she recounts the story. We're alone in the common room. Ruth is downstairs undergoing testing and Carl is sleeping in his room. Dr. Valerie came for Carl's weekly therapy session, but decided to let him rest. She found me reading on the couch.

"It was the cutest thing," she says through a smile. "You were so diligent, pulling up as many of those dandelions as you could find. We had no idea what you were up to!"

She was there, of course. The doctors were always around back then. They'd sit to the side taking notes while went about our day. Dr. Stone and Dr. Madrigal took blood and ran us through batteries of examinations, checking our weight and height and ability to perform a variety of physical tasks. Dr. Valerie led therapy sessions and conducted ongoing assessments of our intelligence, personality and levels of achievement. We were poked and prodded, our lives told on the pages of a lab report.

Dr. Valerie was our favorite. She was young and pretty, always happy, always smiling. She often remained after the other adults left, playing games and reading stories. When one of us fell during recess or got into an argument in the nursery, we ran to her.

She became pregnant when I was nine or ten. I remember wishing to trade places with her baby.

She still visits with us, although less frequently than when we were younger. It's the same with all of the doctors. Perhaps they've learned all there is to know about us. Perhaps they're simply tired of watching us die.

Dr. Valerie sighs. "I don't know how she didn't accept then and there."

I smile. "It's for the best. We were a little young for marriage."

"You're getting older," she says. "Maybe she's coming around?"

"My only competition is Carl," I say. "Although he does have a way with the ladies."

A sad smile sinks into Dr. Valerie's face. I notice for the first time how much she has aged. Lines creep from the edges of her eyes and mouth like cracks in thinning ice. Her features are sharp and angular.

We're the sick ones, but everybody here suffers.

#

In my earliest memories, twelve of us lived in the lab. The common room looked like a nursery then, decorated in bright reds, yellows, greens and blues, characters from Sesame Street and Dr. Seuss smiling down from the walls. We sat in beanbags and little plastic chairs and listened as a Dr. Valerie read us stories. We learned numbers and letters, listened to music and did arts and crafts. Scattered toys, promises of sprained ankles, littered the floor.

Ian fell ill first. He developed a cough that became uncontrollable. The doctors kept him in his room while the rest of us played. Eventually, they told us he wouldn't return.

Angelika, a skinny girl with red hair and freckles, collapsed the following month. A round-faced boy named Steen became ill soon after. Robert, a boy I often played with during the hour-long morning recess on the grassy campus outside, suddenly moved to a location in the building we came to know as the medical wing.

There were only six of us by the time we reached our seventh birthdays.

One by one, we die.

They used to tell us we had a disease. Our families couldn't take care of us. We were contagious and had to stay confined to the lab, where doctors could search for a cure.

It was Ruth who always poked holes in the story. Why did every one of us have a twin who visited the building? If the doctors could touch us without masks or gloves, why couldn't our parents? Couldn't we talk to them on the phone, or through video recordings or letters?

Dr. Madrigal told us the truth when we turned fourteen. We are clones, created from DNA taken from our twins when they were still embryos. Their parents – our parents – signed custody over to Schilling Laboratories in exchange for money.

We were supposed to be a landmark achievement: human embryos cloned from somatic donor cells and carried to term by surrogate mothers. The research team, led by Dr. Madrigal and Dr. Stone and funded by Schilling Laboratories, would become instant celebrities by producing a healthy crop of cloned children. Healthy clones meant an end to infertility and chromosomal disorders and an unlimited supply of embryonic stem cells to treat disease. Healthy clones opened up new frontiers in medicine.

We weren't healthy. We developed infections, tumors, cancer. We began to die. Suddenly, nobody was eager to announce our existence. They brought us here instead, locked away on the third floor for all but an hour each day, when we could run around in the drab building's shadow. The doctors now claim to be working toward a cure for those of us who are still alive.

Our real families don't want to see us.

They want nothing to do with us.

"Do you think we'll ever meet them?" Ruth asks one morning. We're walking side-by-side on the campus green behind the building. It's early September. I wear a T-shirt. She is bundled in a white jacket and hat that contrasts her dark skin and brown eyes.

Not brown. Amber. Almost like honey.

Her hands are buried in her pockets. Despite the layers, I sense a shiver in her voice.

"Who?" I ask.

"Our parents. The twins"

"They don't want to meet us."

"That's what they say," Ruth says, motioning toward the lab. She spits out *they* as if it tastes sour. "Do you really believe it? How could they love one child and completely abandon another?"

"We're not their children."

"Ugh! You sound like Dr. Madrigal."

I wince. "What do you expect me to
say? They didn't give birth to us. They
didn't give us names and homes and
birthday parties. We're just spare cells
taken from their real babies."

Ruth stops walking and turns toward
me. "You're telling me not a single one
changed their mind? There were twelve of
us, Oliver. Wouldn't one of those parents
would be curious about meeting a boy or
girl identical to their own child?"

"Maybe they're not allowed," I say.

"Maybe," Ruth says. She turns and
begins walking again. I keep pace at her
left. We are nearly the same height, our
shoulders level with one another. I look
down at her hands, still bundled into the
coat. I wonder if she might remove them,
imagining our fingers brushing together.
Walking with Ruth is blissful torture.

We move in silence. The lab is to our
left, a box of bleached concrete striped
with four levels of tinted glass windows. A
hundred yards of grass separates the
building from the wooded area on our
right. It is the same all the way around.
The lab is a fortress surrounded by a belt
of green, with no other buildings in sight.

After a few minutes, Ruth speaks
again. "They should be," she says.

"Should be what?"

"They should be allowed to meet us. We should be allowed to meet them," she says. "We should be able to go home with them."

I think of my twin and his parents. We both have the mother's sandy brown hair and blue eyes, the father's nose and chin. I imagine following them down the path, getting into their car and driving to their home. Sitting down to dinner. Watching a movie in the family room, a bowl of popcorn between us on the couch.

Ruth continues. "Don't you ever wonder about leaving this place? Everybody else comes and goes. Everybody else lives in houses with cars in their driveways and dogs in their backyards. They eat in restaurants, go shopping, wander off in whatever direction they like, simply because they can." She opens her arms and gestures at their surroundings. "And here we are. Day after day. Rotting away."

I say nothing. Ruth tucks her hands back into her pockets and squeezes her arms in, as if hugging herself. She shivers. Her teeth chatter.

It can't be less than sixty degrees out here.

"Let's go inside," I say. "You're going to catch cold."

#

We play Monopoly on Saturdays. Carl, as always, plays with the race car. Ruth and I use the top hat and the thimble. We sit around a table in the common room, wrinkled pastel paper bills and dog-eared property cards littering every surface. I roll a seven and move my piece to St. James Place. Ruth has the other two orange properties in her carefully arranged collection. If I don't buy the third, she'll have a shot at building houses along the row.

"Pass," I say.

Carl chuckles. He is lying on the couch, his head against a pillow. The laugh is muffled by his oxygen mask, but the smile behind it is evident.

"What's funny?" I ask.

Carl shakes his head and looks at Ruth. I follow and see her smiling as well. She looks embarrassed.

I redden. "What?" I say. "I don't have the money."

"You've got a five-hundred," Carl whispers.

"I'm saving it," I say.

"Sure," says Ruth.

Ruth outbids Carl for St. James Place after it goes up for auction. A mischievous grin breaks out on her face as she places little green houses on the orange strip above each property. Carl smiles as I watch her.

"What do you think the twins are doing right now?" Ruth asks.

This is one of her favorite games. She likes to imagine the glamorous life her clone leads when she is not visiting the lab. The type of life we're never going to have.

I wonder about this myself. I once read a book on identical twins that described a psychic link between the pair. They share thoughts, feelings and emotions. After reading it, I spent weeks in solitude, eyes closed, trying to reach out and make some sort of connection.

There was nothing.

"It's Saturday night," I say. "Maybe he's at a party?"

Ruth's brown eyes alight. Not brown. Amber. Like whiskey. "A house party!" she says. "There's music playing. Everyone is dancing. In the backyard there's a pool, and everyone is jumping in and swimming!"

"I don't know. It's a little cold for swimming."

Ruth sticks out her tongue. I continue. "What about yours? Is she at the same party?"

I often imagine the lives of our twins intersecting. Ruth's and mine living across the street from one another, attending the same classes, sharing the same circle of friends. I imagine him having the courage to reach out and take her hand, to tell her how he feels.

Ruth shakes her head. She doesn't share this fantasy. "She's out at a nightclub. She's wearing a cute black dress and heels. The beat from the music is thumping. It's dark inside, but the dance floor is all lit up. She's out there with her friends. They're all dancing in a big group."

"Sixteen-year-olds can't get into nightclubs."

"Mine can." She turns to her right. "What about your twin, Carl?"

Carl has fallen asleep on the couch. He sleeps more and more each day. He is so thin, so gray. Ruth reaches for a blanket at his feet and pulls it up to cover his upper body.

"We're going to lose him soon," she whispers without taking her eyes off him.

I nod. She continues. "Carl's twin is up on a giant mountain somewhere. He's been walking and climbing all day, and now he's at the top, on a cliff overlooking endless trees and rivers. There are many stars in the sky. He starts a little fire and sits next to it. And he just watches everything."

Ruth turns and looks at me. I smile at her. She smiles back.

"We should call a nurse to come get him," I say.

She nods. "I'll go to the phone." As she walks away, she begins to cough, quietly at first, then more violently. It's as if she's been holding it in this whole time.

#

Carl dies in October, a few weeks after being moved to the medical wing. There are no flowers, no wake, no funeral. These are things we only know from watching television and movies. When one of us dies, there is a visit from Dr. Stone and a few therapy sessions with Dr. Valerie. After that, we move on.

Ruth and I stroll along the campus during our daily walk. We circle the perimeter of the building, starting at the main entrance and moving counter-clockwise. The weak sun hides behind thin clouds as it begins its fall toward the horizon. We are silent, save for the rattling cough Ruth tries to hide and I pretend to ignore.

We reach the concrete walkway connecting the front of the building to the grove of trees shielding the parking area at the opposite end. This is the path our twins walk, the path the doctors, nurses and other workers traverse every day as they arrive and depart. It's a path we are forbidden to follow.

I cross the walkway and continue along the lawn, hoping to circle the building again before we go back inside. After a few steps, I notice Ruth is no longer at my side.

She stands on the pavement with her back to the lab, eyeing something in the distance. I follow her gaze, expecting to find one of the twins or some other odd sight. Instead there is nothing. Ruth stares at the same oak and birch trees we've seen from our window for years.

I walk back and stand to her left, crossing my arms and looking in the same direction. The bright green of the trees is fading into reds and oranges and yellows. Most find this beautiful. I know the truth. Leaves change colors when they are starving.

"A few more weeks and the trees will be bare," I say.

Ruth coughs again. Her lungs echo like a tomb.

We watch the trees without speaking. I'm about to suggest going back inside when Ruth steps forward and begins walking away from the lab. I watch her take a few steps before trotting to catch up. "Where are you going?" I ask.

Another cough.

"Ruth, we're not supposed to go down there." The path leads to the only known exit from the campus. We've been told our entire lives not to stray toward its far end.

"Let's leave," she says. "Right now. Down the path and through whatever's on the other side."

"Ruth, we can't leave."

"It'll be just like in the movies," she continues, as if she doesn't hear me.

"We'll reach the road and get on a bus or a train. We'll go to a town or a city, someplace we've never been."

"We don't have any money."

Ruth shrugs. "Then we'll walk."

We're more than halfway down the path. I imagine the two of us leaving the lab behind, side-by-side, seated close together as we're ferried toward some unknown destination. We'll find jobs and get an apartment. We'll start a life together.

Ruth's cough persists. We're closer to the exit than we've ever been.

I want to reach for her hand. She would let me take it. I know she would.

The exit is steps away.

A siren chirps in the opening between the trees ahead of us. A white truck appears, a gumdrop-shaped red emergency light on its roof. It crushes the gravel beneath as it pulls to a stop, blocking the opening lengthwise. SCHILLING LABS SECURITY is printed on its side.

Two men in dark blue uniforms step from the vehicle. One speaks quietly into a handheld radio as the other approaches Ruth and me. "You kids lost?" he says.

I start to speak when the sound of footsteps behind us stops me. I turn to see more security officers running down the path from the lab. There are two men in white coats running alongside the officers, one pale and narrow, the other dark-skinned and squat. Dr. Stone and Dr. Madrigal.

"Ruth! Oliver!" Dr. Stone huffs as he draws close. "Where are you going?"

"We're just taking a walk," I say.

"We're leaving," Ruth says.

She glares at the doctors, her back straight and her arms crossed, a posture screaming rebellion. Dr. Stone looks hurt, as if he's just learned of some awful betrayal. Dr. Madrigal's face unwraps into a sinister smirk.

It is Dr. Stone who first speaks. "What do you mean, leaving? You can't go anywhere in your condition!"

"I'll manage," Ruth says. "It's not as if staying here has been all that great for any of us."

Dr. Stone looks to Dr. Madrigal, who takes a step toward Ruth. "You're not thinking clearly. It's time to come inside."

"No!" she shouts. "We should be able to leave! Why ... can't we ..." A violent coughing   fit   interrupts   Ruth's protestations. I put my hands around her shoulders, holding her up as her body lurches forward. We're then pulled apart, the security officers grabbing both of us and dragging us back toward the lab.

I can hear Dr. Madrigal's voice behind us. "Everything's all right," he says. "You'll feel better once you're inside."

They lead us through the front doors. I see Dr. Valerie standing by the front desk in the lobby. She turns away the moment our eyes meet.

#

Ruth is dying.

She lies in her room, somewhere between awake and asleep, an IV in her arm and an oxygen mask on her face. I can see her bones: the sharp angles of her cheekbones, the knobs of her elbows, clavicles jutting from her shoulders like newly sprouted wings. Her skin is dry, ashen, as if she is slowly turning to dust.

I sit at her bedside. I say her name. Her eyes open, heavy, half-lidded. Not brown. Amber, like a sunset. She offers a tired smile.

"Merry Christmas," I say. I pull a small bouquet of dandelions tied together with a ribbon from behind my back and lay it on her midsection.

Ruth sees them and laughs. "How?" she asks in a weak voice.

"I've been growing them in my room. I was planning to spring them on you at New Year's."

"Gonna propose again?"

I blush. "I wish I hadn't given up so easily the first time."

I take her hand. We sit without speaking, listening to the beeps and whirrs and chirps of the various devices monitoring Ruth's condition. They'll likely move her to the medical wing shortly, as they did with Carl, and Barbara before him, and Spencer before her. The turning of the leaves. This may be one of my last chances to sit with her.

After a moment, Ruth speaks in a whisper. "Why did they make us?"

It's a question I ask myself every day. "Because they could, I guess," I say. "They wanted to see if it could work."

"Did it?"

I don't know how to answer. A scientist would probably say no. We fell to pieces like cheap knockoffs while our twins grew strong and flourished. Surely we weren't what they hoped.

We are people, though. We walk, talk, and breathe. We tell jokes and have favorite books, movies, and television shows. We are joyful, sad, thoughtful, shy, confident, and insecure. We fear dying.

We love.

"It worked," I say. "We're too awesome to be ignored."

She smiles. "It would have been fun."

"What's that?"

"You and me. Running away. I would have liked that."

"I would have liked it, too."

"I wish there were more time," Ruth says in a whisper. "I didn't see it until now. You always knew, but I didn't see."

The nurse comes in and asks me to leave. I wipe a tear from Ruth's cheek with my thumb and look into her eyes. She is falling back to sleep. The nurse will soon give her medication, and Ruth will sink deeper into her slumber.

I lean in and kiss Ruth on the cheek. I wonder if she feels it, if she wishes I had done it long before. If I'll ever be able to do it again.

#

It snowed last night. The campus sleeps under a thin blanket of white. I remember a time when there were many visitors here, especially on the second Saturday, the day the twins came. Snow meant shoveled walkways, meandering footprints, snow angels. A landscape of traces.

It is late morning on visiting day, and the snow is undisturbed. Nobody comes anymore. The twins. The parents. Even some of the doctors and staff seem to have slipped away. It is as if this entire place is being forgotten.

I am waiting for one visitor. A twin usually comes once or twice after one of us dies, presumably for a final examination and interview. Ruth's twin should have arrived already, but I'm holding out hope that she is running late. Maybe the snow delayed their trip.

The door behind me opens and closes. I hear footsteps but do not turn around. After a moment, I see Dr. Valerie's reflection in the glass. She looks out the window beside me.

"It's beautiful, isn't it?" she says.

"They don't shovel the walk anymore," I say.

"Oh. They must have forgotten."

We stare out the window in silence. She seems uncomfortable, fidgeting with her blouse, shuffling her feet. She wants to talk: about Ruth, about Carl, about my being the only one left. I'm not giving her an opening.

There is movement at the far end of the campus. I see two figures walking toward the building, leaving a trail of footprints in their wake.

It's her.

She walks with her mother, bundled in snow boots, dark jeans and a black ski jacket that falls below her waist. A white knit cap covers the long, tight black curls of her hair. I can see her face as she draws closer. Her skin is dark brown and smooth. Her pink lips shine with gloss. Her brown eyes dance as she jokes with her mother beside her.

Not brown. Amber. Almost like butterscotch.

"Such a lovely girl," Dr. Valerie says. "Smart, too. Just like Ruth."

"What's her name?" I ask.

"Oliver, you know I can't tell you that."

I turn to Dr. Valerie. "They don't look up."

"What?"

"The twins and their parents. None of them ever look up. I used to stand here and wait for one of them, any of them, to glance up and make eye contact. But they never have."

"Well, why would they?"

"I would be curious," I say. "If there were a person out there that looked just like my kid, that had my DNA, I would want to see them. Even if I didn't want them, I'd still take a look. I wouldn't be able to resist."

"Is there a question here?"

"I want to meet them."

Dr. Valerie and I watch one another. I've known her my whole life. She is the doctor who cares about us, the one who listens to our problems and tells us everything will be alright. She treats us with warmth, love, compassion.

Except for now. The look on Dr. Valerie's face as she stares at me is one of suspicion.

"Isn't the home we've given you enough?" she asks.

"This?" I wave my arms around the common room. "You call this a home? We're stuck inside all day. We go out for an hour of exercise. You know what that sounds like?"

"Oliver ..."

"Prison!"

"This is the best place for you," she says. "Your immune system isn't equipped to handle contact with outsiders."

"That should be our choice!" It occurs to me that I keep referring to myself as a plural. *We*. As if there were anyone else left. "Just tell my parents I want to meet them. I'm not asking for them to take me home with them or anything. I just want to speak with them."

"It's not possible."

"Why?"

"You know why. You have to know by now."

"I want to hear you say it," I say, stepping closer to her. "Why can't I meet my family?"

"It's so easy to demonize if you don't look at the benefits," she says. "Healthy clone cells can end heart disease, paralysis, genetic disorders. So many sick people would have a chance to be better."

"Why?"

"There are some who believe cloning technology holds the secret to stopping the aging process. Can you imagine? Never growing old?"

"If anyone can imagine what that's like, it's me," I say.

Dr. Valerie's face hardens. "They don't know, Oliver. Nobody knows. And nobody will."

I hear Ruth's voice in my mind. *Told you.*

The parents signed up for some random experiment. They received money and assurance that their children wouldn't be hurt in any way. They never learned what was done with the DNA taken from their babies.

"You had no right to do this to us," I say.

"You helped us learn," she says. "Next time it will be better. You've made humanity better."

Next time. As if eleven dead children are nothing more than an easily corrected typo, a flubbed line, a misplaced decimal point. As if there is a quick, easy remedy for our mourning, our suffering, our isolation.

Once I'm gone, they'll find new parents, new genomes to steal from embryos, new surrogates willing to carry them for a paycheck. A new set of clones will hatch.

I hope it is better for them.

"I've got an appointment downstairs," she says. "I'll check back later. Try to get some rest."

I turn back to the window as she walks away. She'll pretend this discussion never happened the next time she visits. It's easier to act as if this is normal, that locking sick children away in a prison disguised as a laboratory is a normal existence.

Ruth's twin has disappeared into the entrance below. Mine will be along before long. I've watched them pass one another on the path more times than I can count. They've never so much as glanced at one another.

I think of my fantasy about our twins being neighbors, classmates, even friends. I imagine their eyes meeting as they pass near the entrance. They'll stop and talk. They'll wonder at how they never noticed one another here at the lab before. They'll gossip about friends and teachers. They'll smile and laugh.

They will hold hands.

They will walk down the path leading away from the lab together.

And nobody will stop them.

See Gregory Kane's story "Twins" online at Metaphorosis.
If you liked it, leave a comment. Authors love that!
Remember to subscribe to our e-mail updates so you'll know when new stories are posted.

About the story

The inspiration for "Twins" came from a discussion with my Biology students about Dolly the sheep. She made headlines in the late 1990s when scientists cloned her using a process called somatic cell nuclear transfer. Basically, DNA was taken from a body cell in a living sheep, placed in an empty egg cell and carried to term by a surrogate. Many students were surprised to learn that she and other cloned animals that followed often suffered early deaths compared to their "twins." My students wondered if it was fair to create an animal if the research suggested an abbreviated life of illness.

I decided to write a story from the perspective of human clone teenagers. How would it feel to have perfectly healthy twins with normal lives and normal families while the clones watch one another dying in a laboratory? Would they be angry? Sad? Jealous? Would they long for a family and connections outside their confinement? As I began writing, I quickly discovered my main character suffered from an affliction common among all teenagers: he was lovesick. My narrative about children engineered by science was actually a love story.

"Twins" allowed me to look at the potential pitfalls of scientific experimentation as we enter an era of infinite possibilities. Human cloning, after all, isn't a theoretical concept. It could be done today if it were deemed ethically responsible. The story created an opportunity to explore how humanity and science can often intersect, sometimes with unfortunate consequences.

A question for the author

Q: What is your favorite short story?

A: My favorite of the classics is Ray Bradbury's "There Will Come Soft Rains." The tale of a robotic household going about its daily routine after humanity has been decimated by an atomic bomb remains one of literature's great cautionary tales. My favorite contemporary story is Ted Chiang's "Tower of Babylon", a dreamy tale of the construction of a tower that reaches the heavens. I love this story for its surreal style and its mind-bending ending, which carries a strong message about human endeavor.

About the author

Gregory Kane teaches high school science outside Philadelphia, where he lives with his wife and daughter. He writes fiction and brews beer when he is not in the classroom. He believes Ray Bradbury's face should be on a form of U.S. currency.

gregoryakane.wordpress.com, @GregoryAKane

The Astronaut Tier

Jonathan Laidlow

Farren opened the door to the bailiffs and let them in. They pushed into the apartment wordlessly, and began to itemise her former life, ticking boxes on clipboards while they opened drawers and rifled shelves. The last to enter was a wiry middle-aged woman who, with a kind smile, invited Farren to sign, thus demonstrating her understanding that her possessions were now the property of Ares II's creditors.

She asked if the coffee in the pot also now belonged to the creditors.

"The coffee?" the officious lady replied. "No. Drink it up, hon. We'll take the pot when you're done."

Farren filled her mug and then added her signature. It was just another piece of paper; she'd signed so many for Ares II, what was one more?

Everything the bailiffs touched, they colonised. The framed prints of movie posters for *Apollo 13* and *The Martian* had belonged to a different Farren, an earlier version, and so giving them up felt like nothing at all.

The coffee had stewed, so she left it. *Let them have the dirty mug.* She picked up the holdall containing those personal items she was permitted to keep, then stopped to allow the boss-lady to rifle through it. On command, she emptied her pockets.

They patted her down and questioned her about the phone, registered to her brother, and the key to the car owned by her mother. They confiscated her old cassette Walkman with its headphones and her box of mixtapes. The male bailiff said, "Vintage! You were cool, lady." He wrapped it carefully in bubble-wrap and added it to a box.

The clothes and toiletries in her bag seemed to pass whatever test this had become. Or maybe she had failed, and just hadn't realised. She waited for them to manhandle the television out into their van, then stepped outside.

She had been renting the apartment for a few years prior to Ares, so she was surprised to feel nothing as she handed over the key. It should have felt more like home, but then nothing did anymore.

The battered Ford was parked down the hill, along the old dry-stone wall of the village post office. She hoped they'd watch her go and think well of her, saying to each other, "Didn't cry, didn't beg or try to smuggle her shit out. That's how you get repossessed with style. Classy."

She stifled a sob on the steering wheel. How had she come from the dome in Australia to being homeless in the north of England?

She recovered herself enough to start the engine and pull out into the road. In the rear-view mirror, she could see the repo boss-lady standing on top of the hill. She couldn't see her former home, and for that she was thankful.

#

Farren's mum had encouraged her to sell all her belongings to friends and family rather than let them be taken, but that wasn't how it worked. The bailiffs would have argued she didn't have the right to sell them, then sued her friends to recover them.

The car from her mother had been an act of kindness, as had the phone from her brother. Not so long ago, in the dome, she would have rejected their attempts to buy back her love. Now she was just happy to have a place to go. She set off to her mother's house, and turned on the radio.

She listened to a call-in show as she drove. The topic was the Ares II project. Most listeners couldn't understand how anyone had believed that a crowd-funded mission to land on Mars was possible, or worth joining. Farren understood, though.

A caller from Exeter said that the Ares people — people like Farren — were despicable, and had joined the project knowingly. Farren snorted at the absurdity, inviting the radio to look around at her worldly possessions and then tell her she was a devious bitch who'd known exactly what she was getting into. She turned the radio off in anger, then immediately turned it back on.

An internet caller from Missouri opined that the cover-up was massive, and went as high as the 'Secret World Government'. "Well I thank you for your charitable thoughts, mister!" Farren said aloud to the empty car. Every day of her life before she joined Areas had felt like she was slowly being poisoned, and so she forced herself to listen every day, to try to understand whether it was all a lie.

The presenter interrupted the callers to go live to the siege in the Australian desert. Nothing had happened, or changed. It was wasted airtime, really. They must surely be getting tired of Ares II by day forty?

Farren braked to avoid a rogue sheep. It was drawn and frail, and stumbled off the tarmac slowly. She slowed again to clatter over the cattle grid and then accelerated up the hill and onto the fells. They had always been desolate, but the blight made everything far worse. There were patches of lifeless soil where once there had been gorse.

The phone rang, so she drew to a halt and flipped it open, saw that it was her brother, and answered.

"Jeff, hi. Yeah. Just gone. On my way to see Mum, taking the shortcut over the fells."

They talked for a few minutes, but everything he said felt like a platitude that she'd already heard. Jeff's voice crackled as the signal degraded and eventually she dropped the phone onto the passenger seat and set off again, concentrating on making each turn as the road meandered its way up, round and over the mountain. She regretted not listening to the end of the phone-in, no matter how infuriating it would have been.

It was dark when she crossed the cattle grid on the other side and entered the village where her mother lived. The old Ford spluttered as she changed into first gear and she felt a pang of concern as she manoeuvred it tightly into a space near her mum's Land Rover. The car was her home now, she thought.

Farren let herself in and found her mother in front of the television, watching the latest rolling updates from the dome. It was one thing for Farren to listen and watch obsessively – she had been there, been part of Ares – it was quite another for her own mother to gawk.

"Mum!" she said, "Can't we just live for five minutes without seeing what those cretins are saying?"

Her mum raised her eyebrows, then got up and kissed Farren on the cheek, asking in her soft Geordie accent, "Tea, pet?"

While the sixty-year old bustled around the kitchen, Farren turned off the sound on the television. Her mother returned with two mugs and a plate of biscuits.

"Did you ever meet that Director fella, the one with the beard and the sexy voice?"

"Mum."

She had indeed met Doyle, repeatedly. Once her application to join the project had been accepted, she had been invited to pay for a seminar where Doyle had talked about the desert installation and the crew preparing to simulate life on Mars there. After that she was invited, for another fee, to an exclusive testing event where the crew for the second training and evaluation installation was to be chosen. She'd lived in the Martian simulation dome for three months, learning hydroponics, basic engineering, agriculture, and how to handle space technology. She was supposed to be in

Alaska now, for another fee, of course. Her contributions had raised her to the Astronaut Tier.

In keeping with the crowd-sourcing ethos of the project, Doyle had pitched in with the recruits and sponsors. He spent weeks in the dome, venturing outside only to attend to corporate business, procurement meetings with companies like Lockheed and Virgin Galactic, and the like. She'd come to think of him as a mentor: he'd often taken the same work details as her, and her posting in the Vacuum Survival team had meant they worked side by side. Her mum might have thought he was dishy, but Farren's relationship with him had always been purely professional. What she'd admired had been his leadership of the project, and what she'd really approved of had been his vision of the people bootstrapping themselves into space, independent of national interests.

Farren thought the harassment charges were trumped up, and the warrant for his arrest a case of blatant Assangeing.

The biscuits were home-cooked, the tea reassuring. Mum filled her in on her cousins and the various illnesses of her aunts and uncles. Farren responded with innocuous childhood memories of the cousins — once, twice, and thrice removed — whom she barely knew as adults.

The coverage of Ares II moved to aerial shots of the compound, then studio discussion of the fire and the first shootout. Farren picked up the remote and turned on the subtitles. The fire was at the mysterious silver 'doughnut' building. She'd never had clearance. You had to be on the Mission Specialist Tier to get inside there. They cut to an investigative journalist, with shots of the Alaskan compound, unfinished and deserted. There was another silver structure, this one incomplete, and federal investigators were shown climbing over the half-built walls with clipboards and flashlights.

While her mum droned on and on about the medical complications currently affecting Uncle Somebody-Or-Other, Farren took stock. She had been convinced that six months in the cold in a simulated space habitat would eventually take her off-world. Instead, she was back in her mother's house and the country she'd been trying to leave since she was a child.

A British scientist came on screen to offer an expert viewpoint. She explained that the designs for the interplanetary vehicle that, it now transpired, had never been constructed, were fundamentally flawed, and the craft would have killed every astronaut upon take-off if they'd ever had the funds to build it. The money taken from "Martianauts" like Farren had vanished, and now they were liable for Ares' debts through some quirk of their contracts. Doyle had been in regular contact with everyone in the group right up until the media exposé and the ensuing raids. Would he get back in touch?

She heard the back door, then her brother's voice, "Hello! Fozzy Bear here yet?"

"I'm here, Juicy," she called back. Then, "Why are you bothering your dear old mum on this fine northern evening?"

Jeff stood in the doorway, rain dripping from his long white hair. "Are you having a laugh?" he replied. "Looking for my poor destitute sister, I'll have you know!"

He sat down, and let Mum scurry around making more tea. Jeff was older by three years. He'd never been a particularly protective sibling, offering her wisdom and perspective when she needed it, but never rushing to impose. He had, however, been strongly opposed to Ares II. He'd identified with their goals, but hated their secrecy and the personality cult that followed Doyle everywhere. He had scoffed when she talked about making the application, and refused to help out when she made the personal video required of all applicants. He'd said that space travel was not a TV-talent show, nor should anyone sell the rights to such a programme. As she gradually got more involved with the meetings and the levels, they had clashed repeatedly, and eventually ceased to speak.

Since the day she'd called him from LAX and begged for help to get home, Jeff had treated her with kid gloves, helping where he could, like getting the phone, and he'd looked after her flat all that time she was away. Now he offered more assistance.

"If you don't want to stay here, you can come over and take our couch, sis."

He owned a bungalow with his wife in the village. It was cramped with the two children, but had always felt like a refuge to Farren. Even when they weren't speaking, she'd visited her nieces and hung out with Sara. It felt like home. But it wasn't, and the thought of living in the same village as Mum and everybody they had grown up with filled her with dread. Sleeping in the astronaut bunks in the cool filtered air of the dome had been much more soothing.

She needed to go, to go far away. If not Mars, then as far as she could manage. She jangled the keys of the Ford in her pocket.

"I'll stay here tonight, and maybe come see you tomorrow, but after that I'm out of here. The roads are safe again, apparently, and Mum gave me wheels, so..."

"Well my couch-a is your couch-a," he said, with a smile that was really concern. "Oh hey, did you see this?" He brandished a printout. Jeff thought of himself as an old school "white knight," and he was always trying to hack things, discover what was behind the encryption. "Somebody from Ares has something going on. It hasn't leaked yet; I just track these things."

"Geek," she said, and took the paper he held out. A photograph: black and white, grainy. A satellite image, maybe. The rocks and grassland of what had to be a British valley. Standing in the rain, a bulky ex-NASA spacesuit reaching down into a stream. The name DOYLE was spelled out in the font they'd all voted for when crowdsourcing everything was a novelty. Farren had even attached the nameplate to that suit.

#

Farren spent a few more days at her mother's house and allowed her to fuss, which meant that she received many cups of tea and frequent homilies on finding a good job and making no more trouble.

Embarrassed but not yet ready to talk, she ventured out to the library to use a public and anonymous internet connection. After setting up a temporary encrypted node, she ran the background on the satellite photo through a series of image searches, cross referencing against open access geo-location directories. Eventually she had some GPS coordinates: an anonymous valley in Yorkshire. This was do-able. The exact spot was off-road, but she could take the car as far as it would go and then hike the rest if she had to. She deserved an explanation. She had been travelling between the Australian dome and the Alaskan bunker when her ticket had been cancelled with no explanation. She had been stranded in LA, watching the authorities move on the compound on the airport lounge TV. And now this. Was the mission still on?

She drove to the supermarket and filled the boot of the car with dried and canned food, a cheap sleeping bag, a tent, and lots of bottled water. She charged it to Jeff and promised to pay him back. She didn't tell him what it was for, but over the phone she just said, "Doyle". She hoped the line wasn't bugged, but her brother had always been good at end-to-end crypto.

She lit out before dawn, heading for the A66 and Newcastle instead of the more direct route to Yorkshire. She had a reputation for aggressive driving, so she deliberately drove like her instructor had wanted her to, like Jeff the family man, so that she wasn't pulled over.

There was a service area that looked down on the River Tyne and the burned-out ruins of Newcastle, so she stopped to rest. She'd seen no obvious signs that she had a tail, and she didn't think a drone would have the range to follow her. If they had enough clout to use satellite tracking, well, there was nothing she could do about it. She wasn't sure whether the bailiffs would pursue her for money, or leads on Doyle. Some people thought the repo company had been working for the government, and it was odd that the British authorities hadn't yet questioned her.

She called Jeff, just to make sure he'd talked to Mum. After pleasantries and reassurance that Mum knew she was safe, he said, "There was a bit more on the Darknet. Conspiracy nuts, to be fair, but there's a buzz about Doyle, so be careful." Then, "Did you know they had guns, Fozz?"

"Don't be silly. I was gonna be an astronaut, not a space marine!" she laughed.

Of course, they'd all had weapons training: daily target practice in the secret caves under the dome and weekly asymmetrical tactical response through the arable zones. She wanted to tell him, but the words would not come. There were no words for the way Ares II had changed her life.

"If you need me — I'm sending a digital key — you can get a message to me without being traced. Use it if you have to." She laughed it off, but he sent the key anyway. She memorised it, certain she wouldn't need it.

She looked down on the quarantined ruins of the city, desolate but no longer burning. The daily radiation forecast had been constant throughout her childhood: the blight that threw the country into recession had started here. The eventual clampdown, evacuation, and quarantine had brought the first realisation that she needed to escape.

She ate, drank, and then set off for Yorkshire, without looking back. A couple of hours later, she ran out of road. The GPS had taken her to abandoned grazing fields, but the location lay ahead, so she opened the gate and drove on.

It was a dull and overcast afternoon and the thin grass was slick with rain. Several times she lost control of the little car, churning up the wet soil and sliding down the valley, but she got further than she thought she would, and she only abandoned it when she reached the stream, with just half a mile to go.

She put on her pair of wellingtons, then locked the car and waded into the stream, splashing against the current. It wasn't deep, and she remembered paddling in the rock pools at Allonby with Jeff when she was a kid and the world was very different. Before the accident at the Scottish nuclear site, before the blight, before Ares II promised her a beginning on another planet.

She rounded the corner and there it was: the spacesuit, walking in the water about a hundred yards in front of her, just as in the photograph. It seemed to be digging or fishing for something under the water. On the other side of the bank she saw a mixture of tents, mobile homes and Winnebagos, all clustered around a long silver caravan. All around her she could feel and hear a throbbing hum, emanating from that last caravan. A sequence of five thunderous pulsations startled her, but she kept on walking.

"Doyle?" she said to the spacesuit.

It wobbled slowly to face her, moving like astronauts in the old footage from the Moon landings. She'd worn one like that and knew how heavy it was under normal gravity. It was one of the ex-NASA designs that she'd worked with at the training camp. It raised its hand, wielding a soil-sampling tool, but she could not find it threatening; her training told her it was meant for low or zero gravity and she could easily outrun it.

"Doyle?" she said again, then, "What the hell, man?"

The gold mirrored-visor retracted and a woman stared back at her from Doyle's spacesuit. She had short dreadlocks and her face was decorated with tattoos. Everyone in Australia had been so well groomed, clean-cut, so *Right Stuff.* Who was this and why was Doyle allowing her to do Farren's job?

"What the fuck is going on here? Where is Doyle?"

Then they were all around her, pointing weapons.

She carefully raised her hands. Behind them, she caught sight of her bearded leader stepping out of one of the caravans.

#

They locked Farren in a camper-van that was joined to the silver thing by a thick trunk of cabling. The motley group all displayed a similar fervour, ignoring her demands for an explanation, but speaking calmly among themselves, as though there was a secret they all shared. She recognised one of them: a guy called Caspian whom she'd always dismissed as a hipster. She'd never hung out with him because he had only reached one of the lower technical tiers. She was outraged that he was here.

Doyle acknowledged her with a nod as they led her past, as if to tell them she was a fellow traveller, potentially a co-conspirator. His hair, once groomed, was long and ragged. His face was lined, but it was still the kind of face that won over investors; the kind that attracted followers and disciples.

The camp was a far cry from the polished Ares compounds and domes. The collection of battered vehicles and aged habitats bore no relation to the branded and logo-ed equipment in the desert. Those had all been leased, she now knew from the exposé on the news. Furthermore, the scientists on TV had said there'd have been no way to lift so much mass into orbit. They had claimed that all those items of equipment were just props to fool investors and members.

The valley was barren, the grass short and blighted, just like her mum's home on the other coast.

The hum of the silver caravan was audible inside the camper-van and it made her restless, particularly the thundering, which cycled every twenty minutes. She paced, then sat on the uncomfortable sofa, and then paced some more. Her phone had no signal. Either they were in a coverage dead-zone, or the cell towers had been disabled somehow. There was one last message from Jeff on there: "Fozz. Bailiffs came for Mum's house. Some legal shenanigans about the proceeds of crime, but it's nonsense. We're on it, stay safe."

She felt bad for her mother's house, but it hadn't been where she felt at home for a very long time.

#

Doyle came to her a few hours later. He wore an ex-NASA one-piece and seemed older, haggard, dirty. *He used to wear such sharp suits,* she thought.

"Farren. How did you find us?" he said.

She lost her composure and snapped, "Where did you go? What did you do to my life? I was on my way to Alaska when the ticket was cancelled. I had to call my family, do you know how humiliating that was?"

He stepped back and chuckled, looking at her with the coldest of eyes. "The mission is more important than any of us. We taught you that. The doubters are trying to take everything."

"You bastard," she said in disbelief. "It was all a lie, all the money's gone and now they're going through our accounts to get it back. Did you know that?"

He sat down and pulled out a hip flask. She shook her head but he waited until eventually she took it and gulped down the cheap vodka.

"It's something else, Farren. Something important. That thing outside — we couldn't tell anyone."

"So what is it?" she retorted.

"I can't tell you, yet. Stay with us. Become one of us again and then you'll find out. Trust me."

"Again? Sod off."

"Think about it. You were one of our very best. But you only made it as far as the Astronaut Tier." She fumed, for Astronaut was the most prestigious level available to the recruits and she had struggled in every way to reach it. Ares II had woken a need in her, and when its promise to meet that need had proved to be false she'd been left empty and desperate.

Doyle's offer scratched that itch. She wanted to leave this blighted land behind, but talking to Doyle reminded her of how much she'd enjoyed being part of something bigger than herself. Of how good it felt to be in the inner circle instead of out in the cold. Now she could be again. He added one last temptation. "Work with us here and you could join the *European Tier*," he said, and his smug smile showed that he knew she would find another level impossible to resist.

She slept fitfully, and then, in the morning, Caspian unlocked the door and invited her to join them on a scavenging trip. Seeing him made Farren sick with jealousy, sick that she was now excluded from something to which he still belonged, and so she meekly went with him and played her part.

#

She worked with Doyle's crew for a week. They foraged supplies from some of the abandoned farms near the valley, then she helped to check the cabling that ran to the mysterious silver trailer. The tasks she'd completed at astronaut camp in Australia proved vital, for she knew how to maintain machines that she didn't really understand. Once, NASA had trained scientists and pilots to live and work in space. Farren wondered whether the lunar astronauts had learned their systems by rote just as she had in the desert.

They were supervised by a watchful older woman with a shaven head and a doctorate – possibly two — named Professor Curtis. She barely acknowledged Farren. Their only conversation was when she demanded Farren's phone. Farren handed it over without a word, or a thought for Jeff or Mum.

Caspian knew little more than Farren, but he shared water, showed her the supplies, and helped her make friends with some of the others. After a few nights, she was welcomed around the campfire for a sing-song, where every melody tried to incorporate the rhythm of the mysterious machine. She found that the others had all worked at different locations and had risen to different levels based on their abilities and their funds. None had risen to as high a tier as Farren and yet here they were. At first, she felt heartbroken that Doyle had invited them onto this new, secret, and exclusive tier, but not her. Then she made it her goal to achieve it herself.

Curtis and Doyle were thick as thieves, but Doyle didn't speak to Farren much. He nodded as he passed, sometimes clasping her shoulder or arm. She wished he wouldn't treat her like his love-struck ex-girlfriend. She didn't feel that her behaviour warranted it, and she didn't want the others thinking they'd ever had a relationship of that nature. It cheapened her, and she was quickly coming to believe in the mission again. It felt right, as it had before. Whatever it was.

Vehicles better equipped for the terrain arrived in the night, driven by the girl with the tattooed face, and then they spent time joining three more silver trailers to the first, until eventually they had a doughnut like the one in Australia. Some began calling it the 'toroid' but Curtis referred to it simply as the Engine, and that was the name that stuck.

They moved into a new phase of testing, and Farren started to show them how adept at such work she had become at the habitat in the desert. They might have been in a north Yorkshire wasteland, but it stood in for a hostile space environment quite acceptably. She ran tests with a battered old laptop and found that the suits still held their oxygen, their heating and cooling systems were nominal, and their radiation shielding intact. The laptop was the type they'd used in the dome, encased in thick rubber and allegedly vacuum-proof.

A few days later, Curtis walked stiffly from her Winnebago to the fire and said, "We begin a new phase of the project tomorrow." As she turned to leave, she took Farren to one side and told her, "Doyle is really proud of how you've joined us. He wanted me to give this back to you." She handed back the cellphone, fully charged. It had even miraculously found a signal.

The phone wouldn't ring out, but then she wasn't sure whether this was a test, and she did not want to break their trust. Nevertheless, she hooked it up to the laptop and used the data connection to scour the net for news about Australia.

The siege was over. Many members were dead, imprisoned or in hiding. The authorities across the globe continued to swoop on the poor idiots, like her, who'd funded and joined what they were now describing as a 'terrorist space cult'. There were lurid claims of orbital weapons platforms and blackmail demands.

There had also been more raids on the families of members, and while there was no news of Mum and Jeff, she shivered at footage of bailiffs in black SUVs breaking down doors and confiscating belongings. What had Ares II done that was so wrong? They had only dreamed of taking the solar system for people, not governments. The idea that someone as ordinary as Farren could have been one of the first to colonise a new world had driven her this far and she realised that her own commitment was more important than ever, now that the state machinery was painting them as criminals and closing them down. Farren felt newly wedded to her cause, zealous to find out what they were working towards. Did they still have a secret launch site somewhere? She hoped they did.

#

Doyle drove into the valley at six with a trailer of cables. He instructed his followers to run them through the camp to a series of outlets on the Engine, and Farren finally caught a glimpse inside the main silver caravan.

The interior was lined with mirrors, and so she saw a vertigo-inducing reflection. The dizzy sensation reminded her of zero-gravity training in the Ares II jet. She had been humbled by the reality of it, as though before she had been somehow lacking in substance.

They had cleared the rocks and flattened out the ground about a hundred yards from the Engine, and they laid the cables to that area. Curtis brought out one final piece of equipment, something none of them had seen before.

It was a semi-circular object, also mirrored, about two metres in diameter and a foot tall, lashed to a standard British power in/out setup with brown parcel tape. It winked and glistened with curious lights. Looking at it induced the same sense of queasy inversion that she'd felt earlier, so she put her head down and resumed work on the power and data lines.

#

Once the cables were laid and connected, Doyle and Curtis began to test them with a laptop hooked up to the generator.

The early evening brought drizzle, and the two leaders worked on in the rain. Farren sat around the fire with the others. There was no more camaraderie, no more singing. "The Engine has stopped," she said eventually. It was true, but nobody reacted except Caspian, who got up and walked back to his tent.

Doyle joined them and ordered Farren to accompany him to his Winnebago. She obeyed without question. Perhaps it was time to join the European Tier, she thought.

As they walked, he called for Caspian and the three of them went inside. Two of the spacesuits were laid out ready, and she helped Doyle into the bulky and dirty NASA suit. She had personally ensured its viability and she was pleased that he respected her talents. "Help Farren into the second unit," Doyle said to Caspian, and she glowed in the warmth of Doyle's approval.

Caspian lowered the helmet over her head and leaned in. "Don't worry," he whispered. They stumbled carefully back outside and waddled slowly to where

Curtis waited with one of the laptops and the new machine.

Curtis pressed a key on the laptop. The air above the new device began to shimmer, to flicker, like an old television set. Farren saw herself reflected in the static, a great, galumphing, mouldy, off-white lummox, outlined in the snowstorm of white noise. The hum and the banging returned, and it sounded as though someone were knocking at a door.

She gazed at her image, transfixed, for she was both subject and object. Then Doyle walked straight past and into the distortion field.

He vanished.

And then the grey sky lit up as though it was morning. She gazed upwards and it was filled with silent black drones, like airborne spiders, hovering over the camp, their spotlights illuminating everything. Sirens began to wail and she saw black uniforms sweep down into the valley, torches wavering as they made their way over the uneven ground. In the lead she thought she saw the officious lady who had accompanied the bailiffs.

Professor Curtis abandoned Farren and Caspian, leaving them by the laptop. Farren grabbed his wrist awkwardly and said, "Open me a link to this location," and reeled off Jeff's key. Caspian quickly entered it on the laptop.

The connection opened and she snatched the computer, activated the oxygen regulator on her suit and stepped into the white noise after Doyle, trailing data and power cables behind her. It was the only thing left she could do.

She closed her eyes as she pushed through her distorted other. It felt as though she had lost her balance, as though she were stuck in the moment just before falling.

Then she was through, staggering to regain her footing on unfamiliar ground. She opened her eyes and blinked in disbelief. She felt lighter, sensed the heater in her suit kick in, and heard the radiation monitor beeping furiously.

At her feet, strange red and grey rocks on a vast expanse of ice, glistening in the light. To her left, Doyle. He stood still, swaying unsteadily. Dominating the horizon were the coloured stripes of Jupiter, the great red storm-spot visible just on the edge of the skyline, seeming only a few miles walk along the icy wasteland in front of her, but in actuality thousands of miles away. The sun was a bright star in a black sky.

She trigged her radio and found Doyle praying. She had not realised he had any spiritual impetus. Ares II had been her own sole authority, yet now that they were millions of miles further than Mars, Jupiter's shadow seemed a far higher god.

After the prayer he said, "I lied, Farren, it's not the European Tier, it's the Europa Tier, the highest level a member can reach."

"So Ares II was always a cover story?" she replied. "That's amazing! We're in space, Doyle, space!" She was so happy she began to cry. *It was all possible, she could leave it all behind.*

He turned to her, huffing and puffing as he adjusted to the ultra-light gravity, a tenth of that back home. "That's right," he said. "Our hackers found the plans for the Engine in an old Soviet dossier. They cross-referenced it with NASA, and that's what we spent the money on. The theoretical stuff is all good and that's why we think they shut us down."

"So... We were never going to Mars." Comprehension set in. It didn't matter where they went in the solar system, just that they were going. It would be impossible to stop them now.

"That's correct. A Jovian satellite! Europa. We can open up the outer planets."

Farren started to laugh. "They really had no idea what you were doing? This is brilliant."

"So much better than Mars," he added.

"Absolutely." She wanted to caper and dance, impossible though it was in the spacesuit. She felt vindicated and justified. It was all worth it.

Doyle said, "Just think what we can sell this for! Portal technology. Can you believe it?"

Farren thought she had misheard. *What we can sell this for?* As she realised what he had said, she felt a lump rising in her throat. She looked at him and all she could think about was the wasted time in the desert, the fundraising, the selection videos, losing everything, her mum's house, the police swarming into the valley — the sacrifices she had made to make space travel possible for herself and other futureless people.

"Sell? What about opening up the planets for humanity? What about the crowd-sourced dream?"

He laughed and his teeth chattered. Their gear was old, and she wasn't sure it was rated for these radiation levels. Red warning lights blinked on Doyle's chest panel.

"Come on, Farren. We can get all the money back. Look at what we've done! It's the Jupiter system! The water on Europa alone can provide oxygen and fuel to keep exploring further. We'll be the richest people alive. The Feds out there? I called them. You and I are only here because I wanted to be the first man in the Jovian system."

"You called them?" she spat back at him. "I thought they followed me. Why would you contact them after everything they've done to us?"

"You're the first woman on Europa, Farren. Think of what that will be worth. They can't arrest us now. We're already celebrities."

The laptop was still in her hand, and despite all of her doubts, its space-proofing seemed to have worked, for the data and power were still live. She roughly pushed at the keys until she hit enter, opening the stream to Jeff. She hoped he'd be able to take any plans and files from the laptop, and then she dropped it and ran at Doyle.

She ran as fast as anyone can in a spacesuit, and bowled him over. The burst of activity set off every warning light and alarm on both their suits. Leaning on top of him, she picked up a rock.

"I believed in this, you monster. You made me believe in this. How can you fucking sell it?" She slammed the rock down, smashing it into her reflection on the golden visor until it cracked, and he grew still.

She struggled off him and sat down, her back to the beautiful gas giant. She looked at the iridescent portal. Should she go back? Or wait for them to follow? How many more spacesuits did they have? How long before they came through and spread out to the stars? Which government would be the first, and would they care that she'd marked their discovery with a blood sacrifice? She doubted it. Her only hope was that Jeff would find the plans and do a Snowden with them. Otherwise the solar system would become everything she hated about Earth.

All strength left her. She turned, feeling cold as her suit began to fail, and looked up at Jupiter. She turned, feeling cold as her suit began to fail, and marvelled at the landscape before her. The barren icebound surface of Europa was like nothing she had trained for, and yet it was everything she needed. She walked carefully and slowly across the white expanse toward the horizon and Jupiter's watchful eye, leaving Doyle's body and the portal far behind.

See Jonathan Laidlow's story "The Astronaut Tier" online at Metaphorosis.
If you liked it, leave a comment. Authors love that!
Remember to subscribe to our e-mail updates so you'll know when new stories are posted.

About the story

"The Astronaut Tier" began life as a story called "Flailing", written for a challenge on the sffworld forums in 2015 with the theme of "surprises in desolate places". I remember I immediately had the image of a blighted Britain, but it took a little longer to find the main theme of the story, which was the Mars One project - a Dutch organisation which was looking for future astronauts not through expertise in astronautics but through social media. Around that time I saw the brilliant film about a woman in a cult,

Martha Marcy May Marlene, starring Elizabeth Olsen and John Hawkes, and read Paul McAuley's superb novel *The Quiet War* about the opening up of the solar system. I wanted to take these elements - crowdfunding the exploration of the solar system and cult dynamics and tell the story through Farren's strength and agency.

A question for the author

Q: What's a typical writing day like for you?

A: This is the dream of the typical writing day: I rise late and drink good strong coffee while looking back through the previous day's draft. I then spend the day adding new words to my latest story and they're all perfect. The reality is somewhat different. I try to read the previous day's draft either over a hurried coffee or on my commute to the office. At lunch I find a quiet spot to sit with my laptop and write. Sometimes I'm working on a story, but a lot of the time I'm doodling with words. I keep the writers' equivalent of a sketchbook and fill it with story fragments, ideas and scenes. You never know when you'll find a nugget of gold in there that turns into a story or a novel. Writing at lunch takes the pressure off, so by the evening I look at the current project. I usually revise the previous day's words before I add new ones. Sometimes I have to go all the way to the beginning to seed new information and events, so I'm constantly revising as well as adding new material. I like to call this writing method "looping revisionary chaos"....

About the author

Jonathan Laidlow grew up in the northwest of England, near the Sellafield nuclear power plant, which regularly leaked. He has one good leg, one good eye, and one good ear … He lives in Birmingham, UK. He tweets @burtkenobi and blogs occasionally at jonlaidlow.com.

Copyright

Metaphorosis Publishing

Metaphorosis offers beautifully written science fiction and fantasy. Our projects include:

Metaphorosis Magazine

Metaphorosis, a weekly magazine of SFF short stories, including stories from all the authors in this anthology. Find out more at magazine.metaphorosis.com, and sign up to be notified of new stories.

Metaphorosis Books

Recent books from Metaphorosis can be found at <u>books.metaphorosis.com</u>, and include:

**Metaphorosis
2017**

**Metaphorosis
2016**

All the stories from *Metaphorosis* magazine's second year.

Almost all the stories from *Metaphorosis* magazine's first year.

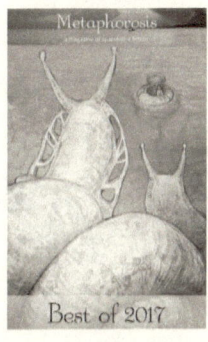

**Metaphorosis:
Best of 2017**

**Metaphorosis:
Best of 2016**

The best science
fiction and fantasy
stories from
Metaphorosis' 2nd
year.

The best science
fiction and fantasy
stories from
Metaphorosis' 1st
year.

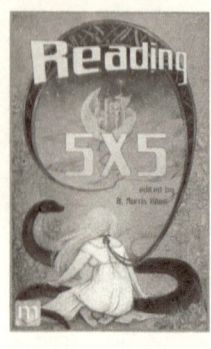

Reading 5X5

Reading 5X5

Five stories, five times

Writers' Edition

Twenty-five SFF authors, five base stories, five versions of each – see how different writers take on the same material.

All the stories from the regular, readers' edition, plus two extra stories, the story seed, and authors' notes.

Best Vegan SFF of 2017

The best vegan science fiction and fantasy stories of 2017!

Best Vegan SFF of 2016

The best vegan science fiction and fantasy stories of 2016!

Susurrus

A darkly romantic story of magic, love, and suffering.

www.ingramcontent.com/pod-product-compliance
Lightning Source LLC
Chambersburg PA
CBHW020526120726
47904CB00003B/980